"I FEEL YOUR PAIN, DAVID AND I HURT FOR you," Bella said.

He went still. With her quiet words, an emotion flooded through him that he couldn't name. He was aware of a soft fluttering in his chest and his breath speeding up. In the light overhead her eyes seemed to shimmer.

He could see two smudges of flour, one on her cheek, one on her chin. Her skin was flushed; wisps of hair framed her face. He thought it was the most beautiful face he'd ever seen, and he had to connect with her, to close the distance between their bodies. What he really wanted to do was drown in her.

Bella could feel the counter pressing into her back as he came toward her. She had no desire to fight him. When he placed his hands on either side of her face and brought his mouth to hers, she trembled. His kiss was unbearably gentle, yet behind it she could sense the power of his need for her, and the effort it was costing him to hold back.

She loved what his teasing mouth was doing to her skin, felt alive and cherished for the first time in a long, long time. . . .

WHAT ARE *LOVESWEPT* ROMANCES?

They are stories of true romance and touching emotion. We believe those two very important ingredients are constants in our highly sensual and very believable stories in the LOVESWEPT *line. Our goal is to give you, the reader, stories of consistently high quality that may sometimes make you laugh, sometimes make you cry, but are always fresh and creative and contain many delightful surprises within their pages.*

Most romance fans read an enormous number of books. Those they truly love, they keep. Others may be traded with friends and soon forgotten. We hope that each LOVESWEPT *romance will be a treasure—a "keeper." We will always try to publish*

LOVE STORIES YOU'LL NEVER FORGET
BY AUTHORS YOU'LL ALWAYS REMEMBER

The Editors

Loveswept 659

HEARTQUAKE

DIANE PERSHING

BANTAM BOOKS

NEW YORK · TORONTO · LONDON · SYDNEY · AUCKLAND

HEARTQUAKE

A Bantam Book / December 1993

*If you would be interested in receiving protective vinyl covers for your
Loveswept books, please write to this address for information:*

Loveswept
Bantam Books
P.O. Box 985
Hicksville, NY 11802

ISBN 0-553-44268-6

Published simultaneously in the United States and Canada

Bantam Books are published by Bantam Books, a division of Bantam Doubleday Dell Publishing Group, Inc. Its trademark, consisting of the words
"Bantam Books" and the portrayal of a rooster, is Registered in U.S. Patent
and Trademark Office and in other countries. Marca Registrada. Bantam
Books, 1540 Broadway, New York, New York 10036.

PRINTED IN THE UNITED STATES OF AMERICA

OPM   0 9 8 7 6 5 4 3 2 1

Jack Popejoy, Ernestine Young,
Lynne Williamson—
thanks for the insights.
Morgan and Ben—thanks for the memories.

ONE

"Come on, baby. You can do it," Bella said, patting the dashboard of her twelve-year-old apple-green Volvo.

Bella often talked to her car on this last lap up the hill to her house. It was pretty steep, and the vehicle had been protesting the climb more and more lately, whining and coughing, letting it be known that it was getting a little on the mature side for this kind of exertion. A little on the mature side, just like herself, Bella thought ruefully.

She'd really felt her age today at Kate's bridal shower. Too much wine, all those off-color jokes. And that male stripper! Even Kate had been embarrassed. Really, it had all been quite tasteless.

And more fun than Bella could remember having in a long, long time.

"Good girl," she told her car as they made the

final turn into the driveway. Along one side stretched a small copse of trees, her beloved rose garden on the other. She coasted to a stop and was reaching for her purse, when a movement to her left caught her attention. She turned.

A man sat on the edge of her porch. In the fading afternoon light she could see him leaning against a stucco column, one booted foot perched on the porch, his arm dangling over his bent knee.

As she stared at him, he straightened and jumped down to the ground. What a tall person, she observed silently. He was at least six feet four, with broad shoulders and long legs. And what a lot of hair he had! It was gold-red and thick, and covered his face too—the man obviously hadn't shaved in a while.

Seeing him in his well-used jeans and faded plaid shirt with rolled-up sleeves, Bella was reminded suddenly of a television commercial. A big mountain-man type, grinning confidently as he leaned on the handle of an ax. Had he been hawking soap? No. Maybe soup? She'd come up with it eventually. With her penchant for trivia, she always did.

Picking up a canvas knapsack at his feet, her visitor ambled over to her on his long legs. Not even his rimless glasses, which made him appear scholarly, took away from the sense of earthy, solid strength he radiated. My, my, Bella thought. The male stripper had nothing on the mountain man coming toward her.

She rolled down the window a bit but, always torn between her natural friendliness and the wariness that years of living in a big city had taught her, she made sure her door was locked.

"I'm sorry," she called out firmly. "If you're selling something, I'm not interested."

The man looked behind him to see whom she was talking to, then turned back and pointed to himself.

"Do you mean me?" he called out in a deep, raspy voice that went along with his rough-hewn look.

"I'm looking at you, aren't I?" she said.

"Actually, I'm not sure. I need to have my prescription strengthened."

A nearsighted thief? Bella found herself smiling at the thought, and relaxed slightly. Maybe he was a sixties throwback with a petition to save the planet.

"Mrs. Stein?"

"Yes?" He knew her name.

"I'm David," he said as he reached the car. "David Franklin."

Nothing registered at first. "David Franklin?" Bella repeated.

But in the next moment she remembered the name and rolled down the window. "But you're supposed to be in Chile, not Los Angeles. You're coming to dinner next week. Or have I got my dates wrong?"

David squatted next to the car so he was eye-level

with her. "Your dates are fine," he said. "I've come here a week early because of that earthquake you had on Thursday. That's my field. I'm a geologist." With a small half-smile, he added, "I don't suppose I could talk you into feeding me a week early? I haven't eaten since yesterday."

"Oh, no, that's terrible."

Under unusually thick blond-red lashes, David's eyes were a startlingly light green, reminding her of one of the translucent marbles her sons used to play with. Even through the lenses of his glasses, they were mesmerizing; she felt a jolt go through her and was surprised by its suddenness and intensity.

"You'd better come into the house, and I'll fix you something," she said, willing her blood to start coursing with normal speed through her veins and arteries again. She grabbed her purse as David rose and opened the car door for her.

He followed her into her large Spanish-style house, where she set her purse down on a small table in the foyer. "Come, let's go into the kitchen."

"Lead the way."

Her high heels click-clacked on the wooden floors that ran through the spacious home. "We're related in some way," she said as she hurried along the corridor. "Do you know how?"

"No. I just know I'm some kind of relative."

"My late husband's second cousin's nephew, or something like that. Which makes you—" She stopped and looked back over her shoulder, having to angle her head up so she could meet his eyes.

David towered over her, which felt kind of strange. At five feet nine inches in stocking feet, Bella was not used to many men towering over her. Six six, she decided, adjusting her previous estimate. A giant. An extremely attractive giant, she amended, even though he was like no one she'd ever found attractive before. Her taste usually ran to ordinary-looking, *comfortable* men. They'd just met, but she felt strongly that David was not a comfortable man. He was too . . . potent for that.

Dragging her eyes away from his and back to reality, she said, "Some kind of relative. Exactly."

They reached the kitchen and she turned on the overhead lights. The room boasted a center island, lots of light-colored wood and plants, and a huge refrigerator. In spite of its size, it gave off a homey, welcoming feel.

"Now, what would you like?" she asked.

"May I have a glass of water?"

"Of course," Bella said, pouring him a large glass of water and handing it to him.

"Thanks." After wiping around his mouth and beard with long, callused fingers, David drank thirstily until the glass was drained.

Smiling, she took the glass from him as he leaned an elbow against a wall, and, frowning, reached under his glasses to rub his eyes.

"Are you feeling all right?"

"Just a headache," he said. "I don't mean to impose on you. It's just that my plane landed early this morning and somehow I lost my wallet—or it was stolen at the airport—so I had no ID, no money or credit cards."

"How awful."

"Not a lot of fun, that's true. I have a friend here, but he wasn't home—like I said, I'm a week early—and I didn't know anyone else I could call, not on Sunday anyway. All I had was this letter from my mother with your name and address"—he reached into his knapsack and held up an envelope to Bella—"so I hitched as far as Sepulveda and Sunset, then asked directions and walked here. End of my sad tale."

During his recital, Bella had gone from interest to concern to horror. "But that's miles, David!"

"I'm a good walker."

"You must be exhausted."

"I'm fine, really I am," he said firmly, then gave her another of his small smiles. "Would you mind if I washed up? I feel pretty grungy."

She pointed toward an archway. "There's a guest room and bath down this hallway, third door on the left. You can wash up there, or if you'd prefer a shower, there are fresh towels—" She snapped her fingers. "Paper towels!"

"What?"

"I was just remembering whom you reminded me of. There was a man on a commercial . . ." She laughed, then shook her head. "Forget it. I have this terrible trivia thing. Go on, have a bath while I fix you something to eat."

Raking his hand through his mop of hair, he said, "I don't feel right, imposing on you like this, Mrs. Stein."

"Bella, please."

"Bella." He took off his glasses and wiped them on his shirt. Without them he looked about thirty, several years younger than she. As he gazed at her, that amazing luminescence glowing from his eyes startled her once again, making her catch her breath. "Nice name," he said.

"Thank you." She swallowed and managed to smile cheerfully. "And you're not imposing. What are families for?"

Even though it had been a rhetorical statement, he narrowed his eyes as if he were thinking it over. "Hmm. Interesting question."

Putting his glasses back on, he stretched his long arms toward the ceiling for a moment. Lord, he was tall! Standing so close to him, Bella could discern a faint odor of masculine sweat, the kind produced by hard work out of doors. It wasn't at all unpleasant.

David picked up his knapsack and slung it over his shoulder. "See you in ten minutes."

———◈———◈———

Also feeling the need to wash up, Bella headed for her bedroom to change. Sitting on her bed, she kicked off her high heels, then massaged her toes. Her feet hurt and she felt bloated. At the luncheon today she had eaten and drunk way too much. But it had been fun; Kate's family were such a nice bunch of people, and Bella had been a little lonely lately, especially since the boys had left for school.

Next week she was to give Kate another bridal shower at the house. The whole crowd from Annabella, the manicure salon that Bella owned and Kate worked at, would be there, including some favored clients. It, too, promised to be a pretty raucous gathering—lingerie and loudmouths, Bella thought with a smile. But no male strippers.

After she washed her face, she threw on a brightly colored caftan Jake had insisted she buy in Mexico years earlier, before he got sick. In her bare feet—which was how she spent as much time as possible—she padded back to the kitchen, pondering what to rustle up for David. With that huge frame, he would need a lot of food, that was for sure. She supposed she could start with a sandwich. Or three. Maybe a cheese omelet. There was some pot roast in the freezer . . .

"Bella?"

The masculine voice startled her out of her reverie. Holding her hand over her pounding heart, she turned to see David's head poking around the kitchen doorway.

"I'm sorry, I didn't mean to scare you."

"It's all right."

Carrying his knapsack, he walked into the room, and she smothered an involuntary gasp. He was practically nude.

"I don't have any clean clothes," he said, looking down at the direction her eyes had taken, "so I made do with a towel."

Bella ordered her pulse rate to slow down. She was being silly. After all, she saw even less scantily clothed male bodies every day in magazines and on television.

Just not in person. That made two in one day, as a matter of fact, if she were keeping count. How lucky could one person get? she thought wryly.

"Why don't I throw the entire contents of your knapsack into the washing machine?" she asked in what she hoped was a bright and casual manner.

"Don't bother. I'll do it."

"Nonsense. Give them to me and I'll take care of it."

He shook his head. "No, you've been too kind already. Just point me in the right direction."

She shrugged and indicated a doorway beyond the refrigerator. "The laundry room is over there.

So is everything you'll need. Stain remover, bleach, fabric softener—"

"Soap and water should do it. Thanks."

As he walked past her, she noted the firm muscles of his upper arms and was struck again by how very broad his shoulders were, especially in contrast to his thin frame, a fact his shirt had hidden.

His legs were thin too, but with well-developed calves. He had a farmer tan—brown forearms and hands and a red-brown V at the neckline where his shirt usually began. The rest of his skin was a light gold color, with an even paler strip just above the towel line. She couldn't help noticing the tight, round buttocks outlined by the towel riding low on his narrow hips.

Embarrassed again by the peek-a-boo nature of her appraisal, Bella made herself look upward which, on David, was pretty high. His now-clean hair was thick and wavy, more blond than red, and desperately in need of a cut. How would it feel, she wondered, to take some of that thick silk and sift it through her fingers, maybe smooth it against her cheek . . . ?

What on earth was the matter with her? she thought abruptly. Why was she fantasizing like this, treating David the way the women at the shower had treated the stripper? She would be forty years old in a couple of weeks. Shouldn't she have passed this stage?

"How about that meal?" Bella called out.

She heard the washing machine filling up, then David was in the doorway, that small grin of his curving his mouth upward. "Well, now that you mention it . . ."

She crossed over to the fridge, opened it, and peered inside, calling out, "We have cheese, salami. Onion dip? I could whip up a Caesar salad, with or without anchovies. Strawberries? Champagne? No, that's been in there too long." She bent over and pulled out a pan. "Or I have some cold chicken. Eggs."

As Bella reeled off the refrigerator's contents, all that David could see of her was her hand on the door, her bare feet, and her rump as she shifted her weight from right to left and back again. His body's reaction to this movement of hers threw him because it was so unexpected. The woman was turning him on. Most definitely.

When they'd met she'd been wearing a silk dress and heels; her jet-black hair had been pulled back off her face in a coil at her neck. She'd seemed elegant to him, mature.

Now, less than a half hour later, in her flowing caftan and bare feet, with her ebony hair loose and framing her face, those incredibly high cheekbones and full lips untouched by makeup, she seemed a lot younger and very womanly.

What a surprise, he thought. What a nice surprise.

However, he sincerely wished that the dull ache in the area of his abdomen would go away. And even though the shower had felt terrific, his head was still killing him.

"David?" Bella closed the refrigerator door partway and looked at him. "Do you want anything I've mentioned?"

"Maybe some soup?"

"Of course. That's what freezers are for." Her smile brightened up the whole room.

She was quite beautiful, he realized. Tall and large-boned, a bit rounder than current fashion—not that he ever paid any attention to fashion. The navy and turquoise caftan was shapeless, but there was no way to disguise the way the soft material shifted back and forth over her full, high breasts as she moved around the kitchen.

He wondered idly if she was wearing a bra, and tried to picture her without the caftan. Then, in the analytical part of his mind that was always on call, he endeavored to remember the last time he'd entertained thoughts as juvenile—or as lusty—as the ones he was having now. A hell of a long time ago, he answered himself with a silent grin. Leaning back against the archway, he folded his arms across his chest and resumed his custom of detached observation.

Bella removed a plastic container from the freezer and popped it into the microwave. Then she turned and smiled again, her large brown eyes giving her face the soft innocence of a child.

Something in the area of his heart turned over.

"It will be a couple of minutes," she said. "I was thinking maybe you'd be more comfortable in a robe, but the only clothes left in my sons' closets wouldn't even begin to cover you. You're so . . ."

"Tall. Huge. Gigantic. Those are the usual words."

"Is it very difficult? Being your size, I mean?"

He shrugged. "You learn to live with it. Do you mind if I sit here in just a towel?"

After a brief moment she said, "Of course not. Make yourself at home."

"This is nice." David slid into the upholstered breakfast booth in the corner and stretched his long legs out in front of him. An old-fashioned Tiffany-type lamp fixture hung over the well-worn pine table, casting a gentle glow over the area. "Your home, I mean."

"I like it too." Bella turned the heat on under the teakettle, then from a bread box she took out a large loaf of rye with seeds, cut off several generous slices, and put them in the toaster-oven. "It's a little big for me, but when the kids are home . . ."

"How many do you have?"

"Two—twin boys. They're up north at school now."

"Boarding school?"

"College."

"Oh." He revised his age estimate slightly upward. "Which one?"

"They're both at the University of California. One is at Santa Cruz, the other at Berkeley. Close to each other, but not too close, was how they put it. Here we are, ten minutes from U.C.L.A., but they both insisted that they go away, which I understand, I guess. It's just that I miss them terribly."

"And you're a widow?"

"Jake's been gone for three years," she said matter-of-factly.

"I'm sorry. I wonder why my mother didn't tell me." His eyes wandered over the rest of the room, taking in the details—the hand-painted tiles, the magnets on the refrigerator door, the indefinable sense of coziness. "She just informed me that after a month in the remote mountains of South America I would probably be needing a home-cooked meal, and we had relatives in Los Angeles. I'm sort of surprised she remembered. She's not big on details like that."

The toaster ding-donged and Bella removed the crispy rye slices. "I hardly know your mother. We met twice, I think. The last time was years ago, at Jake's family reunion in Minneapolis."

The family reunion. A vague memory came to him then: A tall woman with black hair, two small children, one on either side of her—a nice family picture. It was a warm memory, something pleasant from his youth for a change.

"You must have met me too," he said. "Red-haired, freckled kid with horn-rimmed glasses. Probably reading a book or being obnoxious."

Bella wrinkled her nose. "I'm sorry. I can't recall. There were so many that weekend—thirty or forty strangers. And the boys were in the terrible twos, I think. I had my hands full."

"You didn't miss much," he said. "Families are a pain."

Cocking her head, she leaned a generous hip against the counter. "You think so?"

"Mine is, anyway."

"Not mine. They were—" She paused, a faraway look in her eyes. "I haven't seen most of them in years."

"Where are they?"

"A few are in New York, the rest in Hungary. I was born there. After the uprising, my parents shipped me off to my aunt Magda in the States. I never saw them again. Before they could join me, they died."

Her face took on a soft, dreamy expression. "I was very young, but I remember the family dinners, especially the holidays, as special times filled with love. Family means a lot to me."

David couldn't take his eyes off her, drawn to a quality that had nothing to do with her physical appeal. There was no hardness to Bella, he realized, nothing protected about her. She was vulnerable, lacking any kind of pretension or defensiveness. An innocent. He found himself feeling uncomfortable with the fact that somewhere deep inside, she moved him.

"So," Bella said as she got out dishes and silverware, "you've been in Chile. Your mother's letter mentioned something about that. Why? Tell me about it."

"I was part of a team of geologists studying the Isla Guamblin fault line. I'm a paleoseismologist."

"I think I've heard about that. It's a pretty new field, isn't it?"

"Yes. And I'm surprised that you have heard about it."

She set the area in front of him with a napkin, spoon, and knife. As she leaned over, he caught a whiff of tearoses. Clean and sweet, like the woman herself.

"I read a lot," she said. "I mean, I'm not a scholar or anything like that. I just seem to retain things, words, really, like crepuscular and Zinjanthropus and otiose and—"

"—and paleoseismologist."

Smiling, she nodded. "But, David, I didn't know they had earthquakes in Chile."

"The one in 1960 was the biggest one in this century. But there're earthquakes all over the world, all the time. We're aware only of the big ones." Pushing himself up from the table, he went to the sink.

"What do you need?" she asked.

"Water again. I'm really thirsty."

"I'll get it for you."

Reaching into the basin, he took the glass he had used before and filled it with tap water. "You're waiting on me far too much as it is."

He didn't add that he was uncomfortable being waited on and was allowing her to fuss over him only because, well, because he kind of liked it.

Damn, his head was really killing him. After drinking down the water in huge gulps, he poured another glass and drank it down, too, before he returned to his seat again, slightly dizzy.

When the soup was ready, Bella emptied the contents of the plastic dish into a large bowl and served it to him, along with crusty bread and sweet butter. The teakettle whistled, and she poured loose tea into a porcelain pot and let it steep. "You look like you could use some camomile," she said.

He took a spoonful of the savory, hot soup. It was delicious. He wished he could appreciate it. "Homemade chicken soup. I can't believe it."

Sitting across from him, she propped her elbows on the table and grinned. "Like your mother used to make, right?"

"Are you kidding? My mother would have no idea what to do with a chicken, except maybe to classify it by genus and species. She is first and foremost a scientist. Dad too."

"That's right." Bella nodded. "I remember now. Very brainy people. I think they terrified me."

"They have that effect on a lot of people." He took another spoonful of soup. "I noticed the Sunday *New York Times* magazine on the counter."

"I get it delivered. For the clothes and the crossword puzzle."

He nodded. "Of course. You love words. I had a feeling you might be a fellow obsessive."

"You too?" When he nodded, she said, "I'll bet you do them in ink."

"Doesn't everyone?" he teased.

"I'm too insecure for that."

"I'll tell you a secret. I use those pens that erase."

"Cheater. Do you call the 900 number for clues?"

"No way."

"I did once. My conscience bothered me for a week."

He lifted an eyebrow. "I'm shocked."

Her large brown eyes met his with a warm smile that he returned automatically. What was it about this woman, he wondered, that made him relax so easily, something that didn't come naturally to him. David had no illusions about himself; he'd often wished he could be a more open, easygoing kind of man, but it wasn't his nature.

Still, sitting in Bella's kitchen, chatting, even

bantering gently, it almost seemed possible to be someone else, someone who let people in.

She pointed to his bowl. "You're not eating."

"I think it's jet lag."

"But you're too thin to miss a meal."

"That's how I look, and there's nothing I can do about it. I can eat the side of a house and stay like this. I'm quite healthy, you know. And my work's pretty active. I keep in shape."

"So I noticed," she said, then looked as if she were sorry it had slipped out. "I mean, I couldn't help noticing, with the towel and all . . . Oh, dear." She looked down at her lap.

He felt inordinately pleased. So, she'd checked him out too. Interesting. Very interesting.

He ate another spoonful of the delicious soup, but this time it stuck in his throat. Closing his eyes, he tried to swallow down a wave of nausea. Not in front of Bella, he told himself. Please. It would be too humiliating.

"David." Bella placed a hand on his arm. "Are you all right?"

He opened his eyes to see the tender concern on her face, then looked down to where her fingers lay lightly on his skin. Her touch was gentle as he'd known it would be. He closed his eyes again. That headache was back. And the soup wasn't sitting too well in his innards.

"Can I get you anything?" she asked.

"I don't know. I never get sick, never." He took a deep breath, then exhaled. "At least . . ."

His hand flew to his mouth. "Excuse me, is there—?"

She pointed to a door near the entrance to the kitchen. He managed to leap up from the table and make it to the bathroom, closing the door behind him before he completely disgraced himself.

It was some job getting David into bed. Not only was he ridiculously tall and powerfully built, but as Bella steered him toward the bedroom, the towel that was wrapped around his narrow hips kept slipping lower and lower, till she was torn between trying to save his modesty or her own back. Figuring that he was too sick to care, she chose her back. Just before she got him to the bed, the towel gave way and she was treated to a glimpse of David au naturel.

She tried to tell herself that only a sick, demented woman would lust after a man who had just lost his dinner in her bathroom, but her reaction to his body was enough to speed her pulse up, and enough to make her pull the covers over his long, sleek form and leave the room on the double.

Later that night, after his laundry was done, she brought him a clean pair of briefs and left them next to him on the bed. The next time she checked, they were gone; she assumed—she hoped—he was wearing them. There was no way she was going to peek under the covers to find out.

Was he in heaven? David wondered. But no, heaven wouldn't be hot one moment, then as cold as the Arctic the next, would it? And what about the dreams that he thought were real, words and phrases that made perfect sense as he was saying them, until he woke up in the middle of a sentence and realized he was speaking gibberish?

Throughout the night and into the next morning Bella was always there, a womanly presence that was soft and reassuring. She brought him water to drink; her gentle, soothing hand touched his brow and pronounced his fever slightly up, slightly down. He loved her voice—it was mellow and low-pitched.

With her she brought the smell of roses—fresh and light. In his dreams she smiled as she walked toward him, welcoming him, her hips moving sensuously as she drew nearer, her breasts rising and falling under her clothing. He wanted to reach out and touch the full, firm mounds, to cup them, to feel the points of her nipples against the skin of his palm. It was so real, but he knew he was dreaming.

Or maybe he *had* made it to heaven after all.

Bella tried to sleep, but she couldn't. Just as she felt herself drifting off, her mind conjured up flashes

of David as she'd seen him earlier in the evening—
the springy flaxen hair that covered his chest; his
lean, spare frame, so lacking in fat that the arc of
his musculature stood out in relief; the thatch of
curls surrounding his masculine equipment, more
than ample, even at rest.

She had known only one lover, her husband, and
had simply never seen, imagined, or experienced a
man like David before. Her reaction to him unnerved
her. She threw off her covers and went into the den,
plopping down on the faded plaid couch and drawing
an old quilt over her.

There was nothing that grabbed her attention
on the TV, and, as she glanced around the room
restlessly, her eye fell on a picture that stood on
the side table. It was of her and Jake. Taking the
frame in her hands, she studied it. He'd never been
a handsome man, but he'd made the room light up
every time he'd walked into it. And she looked so
very young that day, not a care in the world.

Jake. Thank God she was finally able to think
of him as a cherished memory. Lately the place in
her soul where she used to mourn for him had been
taken over by a sense of restlessness, as though there
were a new journey she was supposed to undertake.
Only she had no idea where.

She put the picture down and went to look in
on David again. He was so still, lying there in her
king-size bed, she actually tiptoed over to him to

make sure he was still alive, the way she used to when the twins were tiny and so fragile that she was sure she'd lose them.

Carefully, she sat on the edge of the mattress and looked at him as he slept, watching his chest rise and fall, and feeling a strong sense of connection with him, one that she'd been aware of the first time she looked into his eyes. He was a stranger, but he felt . . . familiar.

She wanted to touch him; she wanted him to touch her. It had been such a long time since she'd been intimate with a man. She wanted David's hands on her, all over her, even as she worried that her fantasies were out of line.

Certainly they were improper. In actual fact, she told herself sternly, the man was practically a stranger. They had no romantic or physical relationship, nor would they. He was her guest. He was ill. He was family—Jake's cousin's . . . something. He was younger than she was. Quite a bit younger. The list was pretty extensive; if she worked at it, she could probably come up with many more reasons.

Still, she found herself touching his forehead with the back of her hand, then gently pushing a few strands of hair off his face. He murmured something in his sleep and opened his eyes.

By the soft light from the lamp next to the bed, they hypnotized her with their pale green glow.

"Bella," he said with a sigh, bringing his hand

up to her face and stroking her cheek. Then he slowly lowered his palm over her jawline and neck till his fingertips skimmed the ridge of her collarbone. He held her gaze for a brief moment, then closed his eyes, seeming to go back to sleep. His hand moved down over one breast and lingered briefly while beneath her silk nightgown her nipple tingled and sprung into immediate, aching fullness. Then his hand dropped to his side.

"Bella," he breathed. "Beautiful name." His chest rose and fell with deep slumber.

She wondered why she had remained frozen when he touched her, why she hadn't moved away immediately. Why, in fact, she had felt utterly bereft when he had withdrawn his hand.

The truth was, the brief, highly sensual moment had felt wonderful.

She told herself that David had been asleep, unaware of what he was doing. Or of her reaction. No one would know but her, and whom had she hurt?

She watched his face as he slept. His thick, dark gold lashes fanned out above his cheeks, and the lamplight picked up glints of copper in his beard. She felt his forehead; it was cool. Good.

Surely, she told herself, he wouldn't remember what had happened.

Please God, she prayed, *don't let him remember*.

TWO

"They delivered the wrong polish remover and the sink is backed up again."

Balancing the phone on her shoulder, Bella doodled in the margin of the newspaper and listened patiently as Kate continued the list of the day's problems at the shop. "What did you do?" she asked into the mouthpiece.

"Sent the stuff back and called the plumber. What do you think?"

Bella grinned. "See? I told you you could be a manager if you wanted to."

"But I don't want to. Right now I want to be a bride, and it's not easy planning a wedding and being here at the same time. I'm freaking out with nerves."

Over on the far wall were dappled shadows created by the afternoon sun streaming through the trees outside her kitchen windows. It was one of Bella's favorite times of the day. The coffee-and-crossword break. "Kate, can't I convince you to work a few more hours this week? I haven't been able to replace you yet."

"Of course you haven't. Manicurists of my caliber are not easy to find."

"It's a good thing you don't suffer from an undeveloped ego."

On the other end of the line, Kate chuckled. "Tell me, how's the patient?"

"Better, I think. He—"

A slight sound made her turn in the direction of the kitchen doorway. David was there, scratching his head and yawning. She'd left his clean laundry folded on a chair by the bed and he was wearing a yellow T-shirt and tan walking shorts. He reminded her of sunshine.

"As a matter of fact," Bella said into the phone, "here he is right now."

"Goody. Will you be in tomorrow?"

"For a couple of hours, I think."

"I'll see you then."

After hanging up, Bella schooled her face into a cheerful welcome, all the while searching David's expression for a sign that he remembered what had passed between them. But in his rimless glasses and bare feet, and with his hair tousled from a day in bed, he seemed only a little sleepy.

And adorable, which was probably a word that

had seldom been applied to him, and one he would probably hate.

"How are you feeling?" she asked.

"Okay, I think."

"You were pretty sick."

"That's an understatement." Raking his fingers through his wayward hair, he yawned again and looked around the kitchen with a bemused expression. "I wonder what it was."

"I called my doctor and he said it sounded like the stomach flu, and if there was no improvement by tomorrow, I was to bring you into the office. Although I had no idea how I would accomplish that with you pretty much out of it, and taller than a tree." She sighed. "I miss house calls."

He grinned, revealing straight white teeth, and it took her by surprise. This first real, genuine smile she'd seen from him transformed his face from serious and scholarly to mischievous. Her initial impression of him as being guarded was probably pretty accurate. But that smile of his suggested that there was more to him than what he revealed.

He walked over to the breakfast nook, where she was seated, and sank into a chair across from her, stretching out his long legs the way he had the day before. "It's Monday, right?"

"Right."

"I really have been out of it, haven't I? In between trips to the bathroom, I don't remember a thing."

Thank God, Bella thought. Her prayers had been answered.

She got up and went over to the fridge. "Think you can hold down some real food if I fix it?"

"I'm starving, but I feel as if all I've done since I've been here is impose on you."

"Nonsense."

"I mean it. I show up at your door a week early. Then I interrupt your day, use your bed and shower and washing machine, eat your food, get sick, and get nursed by you." He took off his glasses and wiped them on his T-shirt. "Isn't it time for me to do something for you?" he said, his normally raspy voice taking on a soft, intense edge as he looked at her.

Those eyes. It should be illegal for a man to look at a woman with those eyes.

"Like what?" She held her breath. Was there some kind of hidden meaning in his look, in his tone, in his words?

"I don't know. Yardwork? Heavy lifting? You tell me."

"I can't think of a thing," she said lightly, chiding herself for the direction her imagination had taken. She'd read a sexual innuendo into a perfectly harmless question. Was this what it was like to turn forty? she wondered sadly. Secretly lusting after younger men? Fancying that they were secretly lusting after you?

Pulling out a carton of eggs, she placed them and

the butter on the counter, then took down a frying pan from the rack above the stove. "How does eggs and toast sound?"

"Great. But as soon as I'm settled, I'm taking you out for a really nice dinner."

"No need."

"I want to, Bella."

"All right."

She felt him watching her as she cooked, but she kept her body turned away from him as she scrambled up most of the eggs, adding some crumbled feta and grated Swiss cheese. A big man had to have a lot of fuel. And David was certainly big. The complete opposite of Jake, actually, who had been short and rounded and very warm. Now, why, she wondered, was she comparing David to Jake?

"May I use the phone?" he asked after a while.

"Of course," she replied, and couldn't help eavesdropping on his conversation with someone in the Geology Department at U.C.L.A. There was talk of graphs and tremors and temblors, terms familiar to any Californian who followed the television coverage after the state's frequent earthquakes.

"Okay," David said into the phone. "I'll get there somehow . . . Sure. Four o'clock . . . Great, John. And you'll have all the data for me? They faxed the graph over? Terrific."

When he hung up, he ran his hand over his beard. "Do you have a razor, by any chance?"

She checked on the bread in the toaster, then turned to him. "Only a little pink thing for my legs. Are you going to shave off the beard?"

"I think so. It's too hot."

"Oh."

"Why? Do you like men with hairy faces?" There was that slight, teasing half-smile again.

"I don't know. My father had a big black one, I remember, and I used to love to tug at it."

"Yeah, I had a couple of uncles who let me tug at theirs. One was a rabbi. Great long beard, down to his waist. But I grew this because it's a pain to shave in the jungle. Now that I'm back in what passes for civilization, I guess it's time for it to go."

She turned off the light under the eggs. "I see."

She felt strangely disappointed, and David must have sensed it because he said, "Unless you'd rather I didn't."

"Excuse me?"

"I can keep the beard if you'd like."

She stared at him. "Why would you do that?"

Gazing at her for a moment, he seemed to be deciding whether or not to answer her question. His face gave nothing away as he said, "Call it a whim." He turned his attention to the newspaper page lying on the table. "Forty-six Down is 'adrenocortical,' by the way."

"That's right. I knew it was something 'corti-cal.'" Crossing over to the table, Bella looked over his shoulder as she set out silverware and a napkin, salt, and pepper. "That would make fifty-two across 'rapscallion.'"

He nodded and printed the letters in bold capitals. "I'll buy a razor when I get settled."

"Wait, I just remembered," Bella said. "I still have Jake's old straight-edge. In the drawer to the right of the sink in the master bath."

David looked up at her. In the late afternoon sun, his eyes were pale green crystals. "Was it the master bedroom I woke up in just now?"

"Yes."

"Your bed?"

She nodded.

"Why?"

"It's king-size. I thought you should have room for your legs."

His face softened. "But I might have made a real mess."

"Messes can be cleaned up," she said matter-of-factly.

As she walked away from the table, David said, "Are you as nice as you seem to be?"

She stopped and looked back at him in surprise. "Nice?"

"You're so generous. I'm not used to that."

"What are you used to?"

"People looking out for themselves, mostly, I guess. But not you," he added thoughtfully. "You're like, I don't know, Mother Earth. Nursing me, offering your food, your house, your bed—"

He stopped in mid-sentence as though he had just remembered something. "Your bed . . . Bella?"

"Hmm?" She was really glad for her olive skin just then, so that the sudden heat flooding her cheeks wouldn't be too obvious. Holding her breath, she waited.

"I seem to remember . . . never mind."

She busied herself spooning the eggs onto the plate, retrieving the toast, pouring him a large glass of orange juice—all without taking a breath, waiting for the proverbial other shoe to drop.

"No," David said finally, "I have to. Bella?"

With what was obvious reluctance, Bella turned around to him, biting her lower lip and looking for all the world like a guilty child.

David fought down the urge to laugh, but he had to know. "Did I—?"

He stopped himself again. Had he been dreaming, or was her skin as soft, her breasts as deliciously round as he remembered? Never one to mince words when he wanted an answer, at that moment he found himself strangely disinclined to come right out with it, for Bella's sake.

"Let me see," he said. "How shall I put this? While I was sick, did anything of a . . . personal nature happen between us?"

His glance went to her loose white knit top.

There was no mistaking the sudden blossoming of two round buds under the fabric. He felt his own body respond with a sudden sharp heat, even though he knew her reaction had probably been from embarrassment rather than sexual chemistry.

She turned back to the stove and said in a strangled voice, "Your food is ready."

"Bella?"

"Do you like butter or margarine? I have some jam here, I think." She rummaged around in the pantry. "There's even some apple butter, if you like that."

She was scurrying around like an ant looking for a hole to disappear into. "I'm not trying to embarrass you," he said quietly, "really I'm not. If I owe you an apology, I'd like to make it."

She stopped her evasive movement. With her back still to him, she held on to the edge of the counter. "Nothing personal went on, David. You were sick, maybe a little feverish, and you . . . touched me, that's all."

"And I upset you."

"No. I upset myself." After a moment she turned around, holding an enormous plate of eggs and toast. "This could have fed one of my kid's cub scout troops," she said cheerfully.

As changes of subject went, he thought, it was less than graceful—more evidence that Bella was obviously not a woman-of-the-world type who could laugh off what had happened. How different she was from his first impression of her as sophisticated. Funny how first impressions went. He found himself wondering what she'd thought of him at first, and finding that he cared very much about the answer.

He also wondered if, having seen him weakened and ill, she was no longer attracted to him. He sincerely hoped that wasn't the case. There had been some emotion there, he remembered that for sure.

And what was going on with him anyway? He was not used to this kind of introspection, especially when it came to women. Since puberty, when raging hormones had replaced math problems as the major focus of his life, David had enjoyed the company of the opposite sex. Over the years he'd made love with a number of women, reveling in the pleasure they gave him and, he hoped, giving back as much. But he hardly ever *thought* about them or worried what they thought of him. So, what was different about Bella?

In the scientific, disciplined part of him that was always analyzing, he decided that his illness had weakened him, making him less guarded than usual, even slightly vulnerable. It was nothing more than that, he assured himself.

He dug into the eggs, liking the way Bella sat across from him, watching him eat. The eggs were perfect, as he knew they would be. When he was three-quarters of the way through, he put down his fork and wiped his mouth with his napkin.

"All done?"

"Nope. Just taking a breather. I don't think I've had a decent meal for, let me see . . . the last thing I ate was dinner on the airplane, two days ago, so it wasn't that. And for the past few weeks, a lot of crackers and peanut butter."

"You should take better care of yourself. You're a big man and you need—"

"Bella?" he interrupted.

"What?"

He smiled as he said, "Do you always mother people?"

She looked down at the tabletop. "I'm sorry. It's kind of instinctive." Leaning her chin on her hand, she sighed. "I guess I miss my sons. And you are a fairly young man, close to their age, I think."

"I'm thirty-two."

"They're eighteen."

"I'm hardly close to their age," he said wryly. "I'm fourteen years older than they are."

"And eight years younger than me."

She looked surprised, and he realized that the reference to her age had just popped out. Was she trying to make some kind of point? he wondered. "You can't be forty," he said.

"In two weeks. And let's change the subject. I find it depressing."

"Do you? That always fascinates me, the way women resent getting older. Why is that?"

"I don't want to talk about it now. Maybe some other time, okay? What else can I get you? I made cookies this morning."

Chuckling, he leaned back against the booth. "What are you, stuck in a Brady Bunch time warp? Every time something difficult comes up, you take refuge in trying to feed me."

"I do not."

He shrugged. "Okay, you don't."

"I don't want to talk about my age, okay?"

"And you don't want to talk about the fact that I grabbed your breast."

"You didn't grab. You were very gentle."

"Good," he said softly. "That's how I want to be."

She didn't know what to do about that comment, he could tell. The expression on her face was one of pure bewilderment.

"I did upset you, didn't I?" he went on. "The truth."

"The truth? Yes, you upset me. But I got over it, all right?" Emphatically pushing herself up from the table, Bella opened the dishwasher and put the frying pan inside. "Now, tell me your plans. I have to leave pretty soon. I have a class tonight."

"What are you studying?"

"If you must know, I'm learning how to quilt."

He didn't want her to leave, or to have this moment end. He wanted to sit in her homey kitchen with its wide windows that looked out on enough trees for a small forest. He wanted to know all about her, as much as she would tell him, and more. He wanted to watch her expressions change as they talked and laughed, and observe how the sun picked up the rainbow highlights in the wisps of jet-black hair that framed her face. And he wanted to inhale her subtle rose fragrance till it filled his senses.

"David, you're not listening to me."

He snapped back to the present from wherever he'd been. What in the world was happening? Had he undergone a personality lobotomy while he was sick? "Sorry."

"What time is your appointment at U.C.L.A.?"

"Four."

"I'll drop you off. Or you can take the other car that I keep for the boys."

"You're doing it again."

"What?"

"Taking care of me."

She stood with her hands on her hips. "Honestly, David, I'm not trying to. I'm just— Well, you don't have any money and I know you don't have a car, and it's difficult to get around Los Angeles without one, and I have one, so why shouldn't you use it?"

Her reasoning and the sweet, determined way she expressed herself made him laugh. As he scooped up another mouthful of eggs, he said, "Why not, indeed?"

❈————————————❈

They had to shift the passenger seat all the way back to accommodate his legs, but soon Bella was piloting both of them down the winding road onto Mandeville Canyon, then along Sunset Boulevard toward Westwood and the university.

It was a typically hot September day and the air conditioner was going full blast in the Volvo. Jake had wanted her to get a new car, telling her they could well afford it, but she felt attached to this one. In it she had chauffeured the boys to soccer games, done her weekly grocery shopping, taken the various dogs and cats and turtles to the vet. After all the years, its interior smelled familiar—boy sweat, Jake's pipe, her own perfume. It smelled of family.

Bella pulled up outside the old brick building that housed the Geology Department. With the motor running, she turned to David and smiled. "Here we are."

"Thank you again," he said, "for saving my life." He reached into the backseat and retrieved his knapsack. "I'll be staying with John Cochran, an old friend of mine who teaches in the department here, until they find some kind of housing for me. But I'll call you as soon as I get settled. Remember, I owe you a dinner."

"It's not necessary."

"Maybe not, but I want to."

"All right, then."

Bella waited for David to get out of the car, but he seemed as reluctant to do that as she was to see him go. An unexpected wave of sadness at the thought of him not being at her house washed over her. What had she expected? The man had been invited for dinner, not to take up permanent residence. But she liked him—well, more than liked him, but he didn't have to know anything about that. And she'd really enjoyed his company, even if he had so far thrown her well-ordered existence into chaos. And even if he did think she mothered him a bit. It wasn't personal; she mothered everyone.

"Listen," she said, ignoring a small warning voice that was telling her to put the brakes on. "I was just thinking. What if— No, you'll say I'm trying to take care of you again."

The look he gave her was part amusement, part wariness. "Say it anyway," he suggested. "I'll let you know."

"The thing is, if it doesn't work out with your friend, you could stay at my place. I mean, not in the house with me. There's a guest house in the back of the property. Before she got married, Hollis lived there."

"Hollis?"

"My partner. In the two stores."

"Two stores?"

"Why are you repeating everything I say?"

"Stop," he said. "Rewind the tape. What partner and what two stores?"

She turned off the engine before it began to heat up and rolled down her window. "Hollis and I own a gift shop and a manicure salon right near here in Brentwood," she explained patiently. "Annabella and Annabella Deux. Oh, and an art gallery that's about to open."

"You do?"

"Why do you seem so astonished?"

"I suppose it's because I had you pictured as spending all day long in your kitchen."

That made her laugh. "Now who's doing a Brady Bunch fantasy?"

He shook his head slowly from side to side. "Guilty as charged. This is fascinating. Tell me about your business. Business*es*."

She looked at the dashboard clock and frowned. "Don't you have a meeting now?"

"You're right." But he didn't move. Instead, he asked, "Do you work full-time?"

"I go in on Mondays, Wednesdays, and Fridays."

"And what about Tuesdays and Thursdays?"

"I work in my garden, run errands, do the books, go to the hospital . . ."

"What's the matter?" David asked.

"Nothing's the matter."

"Then why do you have to go to the hospital?"

"Children's Hospital. I volunteer there every

Tuesday. And you ask an amazing number of questions."

"So I've been told. Do you mind?"

"Not really."

"Good. What do you do at the hospital? Work in the gift shop or something like that?"

She smiled. "You're stereotyping me again. No. I hug preemies."

"Excuse me?"

"Premature babies. I sit in a rocking chair and hug them for a long time. There have been studies that show that being held can mean the difference between life and death for some of them."

David didn't know what to say. How could a person give so much to someone else's child, a sick child at that? "That must be . . . upsetting."

"In a way. Some of them are so tiny, you know they're not going to make it. It can be terribly sad."

"Then why do you do it?"

"Why?" She gave him a look that said the answer was obvious. "Because they need to be hugged. All babies do." Her face brightened. "And I really love to hug babies. The minute I get one in my arms, I feel calmer somehow, like someone's given me a glass of warm milk. My own personal stress therapy."

He studied her face, amazed once again at Bella's uniqueness and her lack of guile. He'd never met anyone quite like her before. "Listen," he said finally. "About your offer of the guest house—"

"You probably don't want—"

"—I accept."

"Really?" she said, clearly delighted. "That's wonderful!"

"If you'll let me pay rent."

"Nonsense."

"It's not open for discussion."

She could tell from his tone of voice and the very stubborn line of his mouth that it wasn't. "Okay. I just thought that because you're family . . ."

He smiled, the corners of his eyes crinkling a little. "I'm barely family, and you know it. Someone on my side was distantly related to your late husband, so I don't think that counts. I want to pay my own way. I'm a little prickly about things like that."

"Why?"

He shrugged. "I've always been like this. Kind of allergic to being dependent on anyone. It feels like an obligation. No," he added thoughtfully, "more like an invasion."

"Oh."

"Look, Bella, I'm a loner. I don't do well around too many people, or too many complications. It's just the way I am." He paused, then gave one of his mirthless laughs. "And now you know more about me than you ever wanted to know."

"That's not true. I want to know all about you. I—"

"You what?"

No, she wasn't about to walk down that road.

Her eyes darted to the clock again. "You're really late, you know."

"They'll wait," he said easily. So" —he tossed his knapsack into the backseat once again—"I'll be your tenant. Good. I didn't want to lose contact with you."

He put his hand on the door handle as though to leave, then turned to her. "One thing."

"Yes?"

"Why did you iron my clothes?"

"I wanted to."

"But why?"

"They were so filthy—I had to put them through the washing machine twice. And then I thought that nice warm smell you get from bleached, ironed clothes would be pleasant when you woke up. You were very sick, David."

He removed his hand from the door and brought it to her face, where he stroked her cheek with the back of his knuckles, just once. "You're so soft. Outside and in, aren't you?"

She made herself swallow down her tremulous reaction to the touch of his hand on her skin. "David, I'm not some kind of do-gooder, really I'm not." She licked her suddenly dry lips. "I like to do things for people I care about."

"And people you hardly know."

"But you're—"

"—family. I know. As long as you don't think of me as some sort of charity case."

"I don't."

"Or some kind of obligation."

"I don't," she said again.

"I want you to think of me—" He stopped and shook his head. "Oh, hell, I don't want you to think at all."

With that, he took her face in his hands and brushed her lips with his in a light, gentle kiss. Bella put her hands against his chest to push him away, but found her fingers smoothing the fabric of his shirt instead. She tried to say something, but the deliberate flick of his tongue along her lower lip made her gasp. A slow heat began to course all through her; she felt herself leaning into him for more, for a deeper, more intimate kiss.

No! What was the matter with her—necking in a car like some teenager! She couldn't, she simply couldn't encourage this. Not in public. And not until her brains were unscrambled.

She tore her mouth away from his and backed up in the seat till she was leaning against her door. Her hands twisted in her lap and she looked down at them.

"Damn," David muttered as he waited for his breathing to slow down. He'd probably blown it by moving too quickly. But that sweet, unconsciously sensual look she'd gotten on her face as she'd explained why she'd ironed his clothes, the movement of her tongue over her full mouth—well, he'd lost it, that's all.

The kiss had been as much of a surprise to him as it had been to her, and totally out of character. He rarely let anything take him by surprise.

Still, he couldn't remember ever tasting anything sweeter than Bella.

He let several moments of silence go by, then he said, "I'm sorry."

She waved away his apology, but still wouldn't look at him.

"Hey," he said lightly, trying to put her at ease, "it was just a kiss. Not the end of the world."

She raised her head, and he could see something in her eyes that looked like puzzlement. And maybe a little hurt? But no, he must have imagined it, because she shook her head as though admonishing herself. "I'm being silly, David," she said. "Of course. It was just a kiss."

He breathed a sigh of relief. "See you later, okay?"

She nodded, and he let himself out of the car, already looking forward to the next time; he would take it a lot slower then.

THREE

Just a kiss.

As she sat in her favorite rocking chair at Children's Hospital and held Tyrone Washington IV against her breast, Bella replayed David's words one more time, as she had been doing pretty regularly since he'd said them. The words bothered her as much now as they had the day before.

Obviously, the kiss had been a light, meaningless, throwaway kind of thing for him. For her it had been more, awakening long-dormant physical and emotional yearnings that she had given up on ever feeling again.

It had also proved that she wasn't imagining that he was attracted to her, at least enough for a kiss. She supposed she should be flattered—the older woman–younger man syndrome. But she wasn't. She didn't know what she felt, except profoundly confused.

Bella sighed loudly, causing young Tyrone to stir slightly and make that baby grunting sound. "Shh," she said, patting his back. "Shh."

Bella wished she had more experience with this kind of thing, this casual sex that seemed to be the order of the day. Why couldn't she be the type of woman who jumped into bed just because someone turned her on? At times in the past three years, when she'd thought she'd die from loneliness, she'd fantasized running out and finding a partner, filling a sad, empty night with a little affectionate lust.

But she'd been raised to attach more significance to what went on between a man and a woman than temporary relief. Jake had laughingly called her a throwback, and he'd been right. She was a relic dating back to a time before the sexual revolution, when the body and the heart were closely connected and sexual intimacy was for married partners.

But David was a modern man, controlled, detached . . . a dispenser of light, meaningless kisses. Even though she had to admit that she was drawn to him as metal to a magnet, still, it seemed best not to take it any further. She would only wind up getting hurt. Hadn't he said, quite plainly, that he didn't like complications or feeling invaded? And hadn't she heard him, loud and clear?

She was sorry she'd offered him the guest house, but she'd be sure to keep her distance. He was the way he was; she was the way she was. Bella was mature enough to know that the classic fantasy—she would be the one woman who would make David act differently with her—was just that. A fantasy. People didn't change, not really.

Just a kiss.

"To you, maybe," she said aloud, then looked around to make sure none of the nurses was looking at her. She smiled, shaking her head. Enough! Enough time spent obsessing about David. Bella hugged Tyrone even tighter to her, humming a little tune that her own mother had hummed to her. The child continued to sleep contentedly against her. She'd use this rocking-chair time to dwell on some other details of her life.

She needed to remember to order a lot more of that French top-coat for the shop; several of the clients she talked to last week wanted the shiny wet look on their nails.

The new manicurist wasn't going to work out; her English wasn't good enough yet and she hadn't understood specific requests from a couple of clients. Bella hated to let people go, especially when it was so hard to find work in this economy. Maybe she'd call up some other salons and see if she could get the woman another job.

Mulch for the soil around the roses on the garden's western border.

Alex needed his yellow sweater sent up to Santa Cruz.

And on the way home she'd pass that discount linen place and pick up some fresh sheets for the bed in the guest house. For David's bed.

David.

Last night she'd left the key to the guest house with his knapsack by the front door. Then she'd turned out the lights and gone to sleep. That morning she'd left pretty early and hadn't seen him, which was the way she wanted it.

Still, she thought as she sat back and closed her eyes.

Still . . .

She liked talking to him, joking with him, trading crossword clues with him, just being with him. She liked his mind; she liked his body. She liked the way his eyes, usually intent and studious behind the professorish rimless glasses, lit up when he smiled. And that thick flyaway mane of hair, how she yearned to comb her nails through it. And his height. Perfect. Next to him, she felt small, almost petite, for the first time in her life.

And the way his mouth fit over hers, as if they were two parts of a puzzle; the way his tongue—

Enough!

She continued her rhythmic rocking, soothing herself as well as the baby she held in her arms.

David was waiting for her as Bella pulled into the driveway later that evening. He waved and walked up to the car, but she was busy looking at the bright red vehicle parked by the front door. Rolling down her window, she asked, "Yours?"

He nodded. "It's a rental."

"It's definitely you. You are the quintessential jeep-type person."

"I'm the quintessential I'll-take-whatever-car-has-room-for-my-legs type person," he countered wryly.

He helped her into the house with her two bags of groceries, dry cleaning, and some parcels from the Linen Warehouse. Setting the stuff on the kitchen counter, he said, "So, would you like to go out to dinner?"

"Oh. I hadn't thought about food."

"It's seven o'clock and I'm really hungry. John says there's a good Italian restaurant near here."

"He must mean Louise's."

"That's right. Shall we?"

Bella wondered if she could plead a headache. Did she want to? She'd decided to keep her distance, but that wasn't going to be easy to accomplish with him actually living on her property. She'd have to develop a friendship with him, a distant friendship.

Besides, her heart had soared at the sight of him . . .

❖━━━━━❖

In the restaurant, a small, checkered-tablecloths-and-flickering-candlelight kind of place that smelled pleasantly of garlic, they each had a glass of wine. David found his appetite was enormous and ate most of the savory rosemary bread that was served to them. When he ordered a huge plate of linguini, Bella nodded approvingly.

However, when she requested a salad, he said, "What? No pasta?"

"Not tonight. I have it only occasionally. I'm always watching my weight."

"I like the way you're built."

She was disconcerted again; he could tell from the way she looked down into her wineglass. "Thanks, I guess."

"You don't understand. To me, you're just right. Since I was this high"—he moved his hand to indicate a height of under five feet—"I've been nuts about those black and white Italian movies from the fifties. Anna Magnani, Gina Lollobrigida, Sophia Loren—women who looked like women, not like young boys." He grinned. "You could never be mistaken for a young boy."

"Isn't that the truth!" she said emphatically, then laughed at herself while he just enjoyed her. She had the effect on him of bringing up easy laughter and a sense of being carefree that was so rare in his life that he couldn't remember the last time. She was good for him.

After a moment their gazes met and their smiles slowly faded, and they found themselves staring at each other, both mindful that a bolt of sizzling awareness was passing between them. Her lips parted slightly as she expelled a soft breath, and he knew she felt it as strongly as he did.

She was the one who broke the eye contact, lifting her wineglass to her mouth and concentrating on its contents as she took a sip. He found her discomfort oddly endearing. In this day of strong, assertive women, it was anachronistic and refreshing to find a woman who reacted bashfully to sexual attraction. Silently, he renewed the promise he'd made to himself to take it slow.

He hoped when the time came he'd be able to do it.

After their meals were served by a cheerful young waitress, they ate in silence. David sensed that Bella was somewhat troubled; she kept her head down as she ate.

"That lettuce must be really fascinating," he said.

"What?" She whipped her head up and blinked in surprise.

"Is there a problem, Bella? Anything I should know about?"

Grimacing, she shook her head. "It's nothing to do with you. It's me, and it's not important. Tell me, why earthquakes?"

"Excuse me?"

"Why did you decide to go into earthquakes?"

"Your subject-changing skills need some work," David observed wryly, but he went along. "Actually, I wanted to be an astronomer, but when I finished my undergraduate work at UMass, the job market for astronomers was pretty tight. So I took my head out of the stars and went into my second love, the movement of the earth. I did my graduate work at the University of New Mexico. I'll get a Ph.D. eventually. It's all one entity anyway—the stars, our world, other worlds. The whole thing, creation, existence, the formation of the universe—all of it fascinates me."

"I can see that it does."

"Think of it," he said, warming to his subject. "Right now we're sitting on a piece of land that used to be a desert. And before that it was underwater. It's possible that the other side of the street used to be miles away, or on top of this one. Between earthquakes and volcanos and floods and melting ice caps, the entire map of the earth has changed several times over. Is still changing. It's slow, in years, but in terms of eons, it's amazingly rapid."

Bella sat with her elbow on the table and her chin propped in her hand, listening carefully. David felt warmed by her obviously genuine interest in what he had to say.

"After every earthquake," she said, "I turn on the television and see the scientists talking about magnitude and epicenter and stuff like that. But that's not what you do, is it? You don't watch a little needle go back and forth on a graph and come up with lots of numbers?"

"I started out that way, but I'm too restless to stay indoors. I like to be in the field, so I went into paleoseismology. There aren't a lot of us in the world. We travel to quake sites all over the map. Then we dig a trench, climb down into it, and take samples of carbon—organic materials, that is—from the various layers of rock. Through carbon-dating we're now able to determine when the last earthquake at that site occurred and just how volatile the area is."

"That *is* fascinating. And you really love your work, don't you."

"My work is the thing that brings me the most happiness. Always has been."

"But David, what about—?"

Bella's question was interrupted by the bell over the restaurant's front door jangling loudly as a young couple walked in. The man carried a portable cradle while the woman held an infant in her arms. As the newcomers passed by their table, Bella's gaze lit on the child. "Oh," she said, her expression softly, sweetly vulnerable, "a little one. May I look?"

The young mother smiled proudly and showed Bella the baby, a round-faced child with large gray eyes.

"You sweet thing," Bella crooned. "Aren't you beautiful."

The baby smiled and moved its chubby arms and legs up and down. Bella stroked a finger over the child's round cheek. "Baby skin. You have the softest baby skin. What's his name?" she asked the mother without taking her eyes off the child.

"Kevin."

"Hello, Kevin. You're wonderful, do you know that? A perfect little boy with a perfect little nose. You make sure your mommy and daddy have a really good dinner, okay?" The baby continued to beam approval at Bella, and she fluttered her fingers at him. "Bye-bye, Kevin," she said, then looked up at the man and woman. "Congratulations."

"Thanks. 'Bye now," the young woman said as she and her husband moved on to their table.

Bella's wistful gaze followed them, then she turned back to David, looking sheepish. "Real baby-itis. It gets worse all the time. My kids get crazy when I do that in public. They say I embarrass them. Am I awful?"

He studied her, taken again with how clear, how unfiltered her reactions were to everything around her. "I suppose a mother who is as enthusiastic and uninhibited as you are would be embarrassing to teenage boys. But no, you're far from awful. You're unique, that's what you are."

"Good unique or bad unique?"

"Most definitely good."

"Thank God," she said, grinning. "I love babies, in case you can't tell. I can't wait to be a grandmother, so there's a little one around to cuddle with."

"You're a little young to be talking about being a grandmother."

"Not really. Just a generation ago, I probably would have been one by now."

"With the way you feel about babies, why didn't you have any more children?" Her expression made him wish he hadn't asked that question. "If you'd rather not—"

"It's okay. Jake was a lot older than me and, somehow, with his illness and all . . . it didn't work out. Besides, the boys were quite a handful, so I didn't have a lot of time to think about it. Tell me, David—" Bella stopped, not sure if she should ask. "No, it's none of my business."

"What?" He drank down the rest of his wine. "You can ask me anything you'd like."

"I guess I'm curious about your personal life. I mean, you travel all the time, and you seem to be something of a loner. I wondered if you've ever wanted a family, children of your own."

He paused before he answered. Then, in an even, unemotional tone, he said, "I was married once."

"Really?"

"For two months. It was while I was in college. She got pregnant and we married. I was miserable the entire time. Then she had a miscarriage and we both agreed there was no reason to stay together."

"Maybe she wasn't the right one," Bella offered.

"I've heard that phrase before, of course. But I think it's me that's not the right one. I've come to the conclusion that for me, being part of a couple on any permanent basis is probably not in the cards. From what I've seen, people who love have a gift, one that I seem to lack." For a fleeting moment Bella thought she saw regret in his eyes. But then he shrugged and it was gone. "It's never been a priority, that's all. I'm fine as I am."

"I guess I'm a romantic, but I think love and family are something everyone should have."

"That's because you have the gift. You were very much in love with your husband, I take it."

"He and my sons were the center of my universe."

"I study the universe from the outside, the way a scientist is supposed to. And I'm perfectly content that way."

In the jeep on the way back to her house, David said, "Tell me about these shops of yours."

Bella was still replaying their conversation in the restaurant, still trying to understand why someone would want to build so many walls to defend himself. David's detachment *had* to be covering up the very human need to connect; didn't all people need that?

"It started out kind of casually," she said in answer to his question. "When the boys began nursery school, Anna and I—she was Hollis's mother—we were pretty unhappy at this salon we worked at and thought we'd give it a try on our own. We put our names together and came up with Annabella. Real creative, huh?"

"I like the name. It's kind of old-fashioned."

"That would describe Anna and me, for sure. We wanted a place where the customer could get away from her cares and get good service in a nice atmosphere. And we weren't interested in being trendy. We found a space in West Hollywood. Kate was looking for work then, so she came with us right from the start. Then there were some others, and soon we had about eight full-time manicurists. It really took off."

"I'm not surprised." David looked at her with approval, and Bella shrugged modestly.

"Our timing was good, and Anna and I always believed in hard work. About ten years ago, when Jake and I bought the house, we moved the shop to this location at the Brentwood Country Mart— right across the street from where we ate tonight, as a matter of fact. It was a two-story building, we put the salon upstairs. Anna had a real flair for antiques, so we started the gift shop downstairs, which we named Annabella Deux."

"If Hollis is your partner, what happened to Anna?"

Bella's smile was melancholy. "She died last year. She was my best friend."

They stopped at a red light. On either side of them, tall trees rose into the sky, barely visible in the dark, moonless night. David draped a wrist over the steering wheel. "You've had a lot of loss, haven't you?" he said softly. "Your parents, your husband, your partner."

"Yes, I guess I have."

"And from what I can tell, you've taken care of a lot of people along the way."

Bella looked over at him. Something flickered in David's silver-green eyes; was it compassion or just a streetlight?

"Tell me, Bella," he continued. "Who takes care of you?"

She swallowed down a sudden heaviness in her chest that surprised her with its strength. "I don't need a lot of taking care of."

"That's my line, I think," he said thoughtfully, then added almost to himself, "I wonder if we're both lying to ourselves."

They drove the rest of the way in silence. At her house, David turned off the car's engine, but made no move to get out, instead staring ahead into the black night for a while. Bella also stayed where she was, unable to get her body to do anything except watch his profile as he watched the night.

Turning in his seat, he took her hand in his, his gaze wandering all over her face as though she had an answer hidden on it somewhere. Then he shook his head slowly. "You have the strangest effect on me. I find myself saying things to you I didn't even know I was feeling."

"Me too. I guess we're becoming friends."

"Friends," he repeated. "First I'm family, now I'm a friend."

A little smile curved his mouth as he ran his thumb back and forth over her wrist. She shivered at his touch.

"What do I get to be next?" he whispered.

"I . . . think we stop there." Even to her own ears she sounded less than certain.

"Do we?"

"Yes."

"I see," he said.

"I'm going in now, David. I'm pretty tired."

His hand cupped her face as he studied her, again seeming to be searching for something. "All right. I'm kind of tired too. Sweet dreams."

She let herself out of the car, feeling his gaze on her back as she opened her door and let herself in. From the way her blood was racing after one touch of his hand, she would dream that night, she knew that. But her dreams probably wouldn't be sweet.

Bella had been avoiding him since they'd gone out to dinner on Tuesday night. Three days. David had half expected her to invite him over for a meal, but she hadn't. Each night when he drove up the driveway, he would look for her, but she was either out or the lights in the house weren't on. They ran into each other once, when she was going and he was coming, and they chatted briefly. She asked how he was getting on, and he asked how she was—surface kind of chitchat, nothing substantial.

Something had gone wrong and it really bothered him. She'd turned off. He needed to know why.

That morning, as he was hurrying out of the guest house, he saw her kneeling between the rosebushes in her garden, attacking the weeds with a vengeance. It was barely light enough to see, but she was dressed in full gardening regalia—a broad hat, thick cotton gloves, and old, loose clothing. He couldn't see her face, but her movements seemed pretty intense, almost angry.

He was supposed to be at the site in Santa Monica at six-thirty A.M.—he glanced at his watch—in three minutes. The new study had finally been funded, and they were breaking ground today. But his coworkers were used to his chronic lateness, so he could take a moment to talk to Bella before he took off.

Walking up behind her, he said, "I'll be glad to pick up some chemical-free weed killer for you if you'd like."

Bella gasped, held her hand to her heart, then turned around and looked up at him. "David! You startled me!"

He hunkered down next to her. "Sorry. Do you picture someone's face in the dirt when you stab at it like that?"

She looked taken aback, then laughed. "Not really. I guess I'm working out a little tension."

"So it seems. Anything you want to talk about? Maybe I can help."

"No, thanks." She bent her head so that the hat shielded the expression in her eyes from him. "I have a lot to do today, so I'm starting out in a hurry."

"I see." Instead of getting up, which he was sure she expected him to do, he sat down on the gravel pathway that ran next to this patch of garden and crossed his legs, Indian fashion. "Can you take a minute and talk to me anyway?"

The hat came up; her face was guarded. "Maybe a minute."

"I think I must have offended you, either by kissing you or by something I said. I do that sometimes, hurt people's feelings without meaning to."

"You haven't offended me, David. Why would you think that?"

"Because you've changed toward me, pretty drastically, and that was all I could come up with."

"Oh. I see." She nodded, then said, "Well, no. The shop—I mean I've been trying to—" She looked away from him. "I've been really busy, that's all."

"You're a terrible liar, you know."

He could see the struggle going on inside her by the way the muscles of her face shifted subtly. She was deciding just how honest to be with him.

Offering one of his half-smiles, he said lightly, "It's all right, Bella. Don't worry about hurting me or anything. I'm pretty thick-skinned."

A moment passed. Then she said gently, "No, you're not, David. You just think you are."

The way she was looking at him with those warm, understanding brown eyes got to him. A sense of disorientation slammed into him; it was as if his feet had been knocked out from under him. He frowned, thrown by his reaction, then shrugged off the feeling.

"You may be right," he went on, "but we were talking about you. Please, tell me the truth. Why are you avoiding me? I thought we were getting along so well."

"We were. We still are. I like you very much."

"And I like you very much. I think you know that."

"Yes."

"So, I would like us to— I mean . . ." *I want us to be together*, he wanted to say. *I want us to kiss and explore each other. I want to feel your soft, womanly body under my hands, my mouth, my tongue. And I think you want that too.*

But he censored those words, although he wasn't quite sure why. He told himself that it was because, even though he wanted to get this thing out into the open, it was obvious that Bella was reluctant to do so. He was sparing her, he told himself. But the truth probably had more to do with the fact that he was afraid. What if he did say what was on his mind and she turned him down? He didn't even want to think about it.

He glanced at his watch, then stood and brushed off the back of his jeans, although why he was bothering he couldn't have said. He'd be spending most of his days for the next several weeks digging around in a lot more dirt than that.

"I have to go right now," he said. "And you're not really in the mood for a heart-to-heart, are you?"

She sighed. "Not really."

"Okay. See you later." He waved and walked off.

Bella watched him go, unable to take her eyes off him. He hadn't had his hair cut yet, or taken off the beard. His torn T-shirt didn't quite make it to his waistline, and his jeans rode dangerously low on his narrow hips. And he didn't even seem to be wearing any underwear!

For a brief moment Bella remembered what she'd glimpsed while helping him into bed the night he was sick, and that was enough to make her face heat up and send her heart thumping loudly in her chest.

She was all right as long as she didn't see him. Well, relatively all right. But bring him into her presence and there she went again, fantasizing, yearning, practically *lusting* after him. Not good, Bella, she admonished herself, not good the way he affected both her loins and her soul.

Something about David Franklin touched her deeply, and she wondered if, in spite of her best efforts, she was on the road to heartache.

"Hey, Franklin, toss me the hoe, will you?"

David looked up at the sound of John's voice. "Huh?"

"The hoe, man. What's with you? That's the third time I asked for it." John's exasperation was tinged with good humor. Since their days back in college, David had never seen John lose his temper.

Picking out the tool from the others in the back of the truck, David trotted over to the other two geologists who were his partners in this study.

"Sorry," he said. "I'm kind of spacy today, I guess."

"I guess," John agreed, a smile on his plain round face. "What's going on?"

"I think I'm working on an equation in my head."

"Geometric, chemical, or what?" asked Chris, the third member of the team, a brilliant graduate student whose cropped blond hair and thin body made her look ten years younger than her twenty-two years.

"What," he replied cryptically. "How's it coming along, you two? Ready for the professor here to lend a hand?"

Neither John nor Chris had ever participated in this kind of project before. Most of their work had been theoretical, while David had several years of practical experience, digging and collecting carbon samples in faults all over the world. He was considered one of the rising stars in the field; his name attached to the project had made funding easier for the U.C.L.A. group to obtain.

"We have a little more prep work to do here," John said.

"Sure you don't want me to help?"

"Why don't you take a walk or something? Clear your head."

David looked around the small, empty field. It stood at the end of a modest residential street on a bluff overlooking the ocean. The colors of the Pacific were steel-gray mottled with turquoise. Sailboats stood out against the light blue sky; fifty feet below, gentle waves lapped at the shoreline. "Maybe I should take off," he said, "just for a little while."

Out of the corner of his eye David saw a small tangle of greenery. He walked over to it and kneeled down, touching the velvety petals of one of the small flowers. Wild roses—yellow and gold and white.

Roses. Bella smelled like roses.

Bella.

He stood up and checked the time. Noon. "I'll be back in an hour."

He took off in the rented car, heading east. He was ten minutes from Brentwood. The other night she'd mentioned that her shop was across the street from the restaurant. It was Friday, and if he remembered correctly, she'd said she was at the shop Monday, Wednesday, and Friday.

He shouldn't have chickened out that morning, he told himself. He should have come right out with it, gotten it worked out one way or the other, then he wouldn't be having such a rough time concentrating at the dig.

This was a very important project, one that would add more data to the present bank of information on the earth's movements, data sorely needed so that mankind could better prepare itself for catastrophe.

He liked his work; no, he loved it. But this attraction, this . . . tenderness he felt toward Bella, it was messing around with his head. He couldn't afford it. His career couldn't afford it.

He'd go to see her at the shop, get it handled, even if she rejected him. It had happened before. Not often, of course; he always made pretty sure he understood the signals a woman was giving him before he made his move.

Bella's signals were of the mixed type, most definitely, he thought, smiling as he remembered her flushed face, her evasive eyes.

Well, whatever. He would survive, no matter what happened.

He always did.

FOUR

"So, when's Kate's wedding?" Mrs. Huston asked Bella. "Will she be coming back to the shop and why are you doing nails again and how are the boys?"

Bella smiled as she finished removing the chipped red polish from the elderly woman's nails. She'd forgotten how Mrs. Huston always asked three or four questions in a row, as though she were calling in to a radio talk show, and then sat back and waited for the answers. Annabella was the perfect place for the plump septuagenarian to indulge in her favorite pastime, gossiping.

"The wedding is the Sunday after this," Bella said, "and no, she'll be back part-time only. I'm filling in till we get someone to take her place. And Alex and Sam are both fine at college, I think. They don't tell me anything anymore."

"They're like that after a certain age, aren't they? Well, tell me about yourself, then. Something juicy."

The old woman's eyes gleamed, giving a youthful lift to her softly lined face. "Are you dating anyone special?"

One of the reasons Bella didn't miss giving manicures was this kind of conversation. Because they enjoyed sharing the intimate details of their own lives, clients usually felt they had the right to hear all about hers. "No. I don't date at all, actually."

"But why not? You're still so young."

Bella smiled. "I guess that depends on your perspective. Lately, I've been feeling anything but. Soak your fingers, Mrs. Huston, while I get myself a cup of coffee. Would you like some?"

"Please. One sugar."

Glancing around the salon—a large, airy room that was decorated in cheerful colors—Bella went over to the coffeemaker. It was a fairly elaborate machine that kept three pots going at the same time—regular, decaf, and hot water for tea. She made a mental note to tell Clarence, her coffee supplier, that the new Swiss decaf was definitely tastier than the old stuff and to see if they could come to an agreement on price. The amount he was asking was outrageous.

"What a great skirt, Bella. Where did you get it?" The question came from a small, slender man who sat in an armchair, waiting for his appointment with Donna.

"I can't remember," she said, glancing down at

the jungle-print long cotton garment that fell to her ankles. "I've had it forever."

Chuck had been coming to the salon for years, and was one of Bella's favorite regulars. As she poured coffee into two porcelain cups, she heard him say, "Well, well, what do we have here? The jolly red giant, I assume."

Bella looked over toward the shop's entrance as David came into the room, his head bent to avoid hitting it on the curved archway at the top of the stairs. As he looked around, she could see what Chuck meant. David's face was quite red; wherever he'd been, he'd managed to get a fresh dose of sunburn. He was still wearing the torn T-shirt and low-slung jeans he'd had on that morning and, the moment his eyes lit on her, her heart began to thump erratically.

Smiling his small grin, he headed over to where Bella stood, holding two cups in her hands and feeling speechless with pleasure at his appearance. "Hi," he said. "I'm glad I found you."

"Hi, yourself," she managed to say. "Is everything all right?"

"Sure. I just wanted to see you."

Bella noticed suddenly that apart from the soft rock playing over the speakers, the usual background noise in the shop had diminished almost totally. She looked around to see all nine manicurists and their customers watching her and David with obvious relish.

Noticing it too, David asked, "Is there some-where you and I can talk?"

"I'm in the middle of a manicure."

"Oh, I didn't know . . ."

He looked so disappointed that she said, "But I can take two minutes, okay?" Setting her own cup down, Bella added a spoonful of sugar to the other and took it over to Mrs. Huston, who had been regarding the two of them with avid, birdlike interest.

David watched Bella as she walked, noting with pleasure the movement of her skirt as her hips swayed back and forth. As she leaned over to speak to her customer, David couldn't tear his eyes away from her. Above the skirt she wore a dark green jersey top and wide black belt, and her hair was pulled off her face by a tortoiseshell barrette worn low on her neck. In her large gold hoop earrings and thin-strapped black sandals, she reminded him of a sophisticated, sensual Gypsy.

Suddenly he felt less sure of what he would say to her. Two minutes to talk. What could he cover in two minutes? *Hey baby, I want you. How does that strike you?* Damn. Like something out of a bad movie. He shook his head. Two minutes, indeed. No way, not with this woman. This kind of thing needed time—soft lights, wine, patience.

This kind of thing, he repeated to himself. The phrase resonated strangely, somehow. What kind

of thing was he talking about? All that was going
on was chemistry—that certain something that happened between a man and a woman when two sets
of hormones spontaneously reached for each other.
It was there. Either she wanted to act on it or she
didn't. But still, it was only chemistry.

Tell me another one, he chided himself as she
walked toward him. It was more than simple chemistry, and he knew it. The woman got to him like no
one ever had before. She saw things in him that he
never let anyone else see, the stuff below the surface.
She was special.

She touched him.

David followed Bella into a small kitchen. "Have
one," she said, bringing over a platter of oatmeal
cookies from the counter.

She was offering food again, he observed silently.
A definite sign. She sat herself down at the white ice
cream table in the corner and he did the same, realizing as he bit into the cookie that he hadn't eaten
yet that day. "These are delicious."

"Thanks," she said. "I made them last night."

"Really? I walked by the kitchen about ten and
there were no lights on."

"I mean later. About three."

"In the morning? Why so late?"

Shrugging, she said, "I have these occasional
nights when I can't sleep."

"Yeah. I know what you mean."

While one part of her engaged in casual conversation, Bella watched him, watched the motion of David's bearded jawline as he chewed, as his tongue darted out to lick a few stray crumbs from the corner of his mouth. When he finished, he brought his bottom lip up over his mustache and captured a couple of oatmeal flakes. She followed the movement of his hand as he reached for another cookie and made quick work of it.

Could he tell, she wondered, that every aspect of him fascinated her? That she was as drawn to him as was a flower reaching toward sunlight? It was a difficult thing to hide, though she'd certainly been trying. But, darn it, she liked it that he liked her baking, that he had popped in to see her in the middle of the day. She liked that very much.

"These are really good." He took another cookie. "Last one, promise."

"Take them all if you want."

"What? And spoil my appetite?"

Smiling, she asked, "Haven't you eaten?"

"I'm grabbing lunch right after this. I don't suppose you can join me."

"I can't. I have another appointment after this one, then I'm interviewing a couple of manicurists. I sure hope I can replace Kate soon. So, what did you want to talk to me about?"

David wiped around his mouth with his thumb and finger, smoothing down his beard and mustache as he did. He had that look on his face that she was starting to recognize, the one that said he was working something out in that complicated brain of his.

"I found myself thinking about you this morning," he said finally. "So I came here on an impulse."

"What a nice impulse. Where were you?"

"In Santa Monica. We're starting a new project there."

Bella fought the sudden urge to push a few stray strands of hair back from his face. Propping her elbow on the table, she leaned her hand on her chin. "You should probably watch out for the sun. The California climate can be deceptive."

He touched his cheek with the back of his hand, feeling his skin's heat. "I guess I forgot to put on sunscreen this morning. I've been forgetting a lot of things lately. It's not like me." Looking down at the table, he said, "That's what I wanted to talk to you about. The thing is—"

He stopped, then seemed to be debating something in his mind as he picked up a couple of cookie crumbs from the table and flicked them onto the platter. Shaking his head, he said almost to himself, "No, not now. Bad timing."

Then he looked directly at her. "Tonight. Will you be home tonight?"

His eyes, those glowing green crystals, were impossible to resist. "Yes," she replied, abandoning her foolish plan of avoiding contact with him. Who was she kidding?

"Good. I'll see you then." He rose from the table and stood over her, startling her momentarily with how far back she had to crane her neck to see his face. "Is there a hamburger stand near here?"

"Go down the stairs, through the gift shop, and turn left. You'll see a bunch of different food stalls in the courtyard. I particularly recommend the barbecue chicken place. The french fries are the best in town."

He grinned at her, the happy grin, the one that revealed the eager, open young man beneath the detached scientist. She felt like laughing out loud.

"Good news for a french fry junkie," he said. "See you later tonight?"

"I'll be there. Come to the back kitchen door. I have a lot of baking to do."

Leaning a hip against the door frame, she watched as he crossed the small room on long, lanky legs. At the top of the stairs he turned around to say good-bye one last time and managed to bump his head. "Ouch."

Bella rushed over to him, her hand covering her mouth. Wincing, David shook his head ruefully.

"Are you all right?" she asked.

He rubbed his callused fingers over a spot on his forehead. "It's funny about genetic pools. Both of my parents are average height. My father is even shorter than average. But somewhere on both sides there are very tall men—Uncle Phil and Uncle Henry— and they sure left their stamp on me. Anyway, yes, I'm fine."

He studied her for a moment longer, then lightly touched the tip of her nose with his finger. "See you later." Carefully ducking his head, he went down the stairs.

As Bella turned back to the room, Chuck came up to her and placed her abandoned coffee cup in her hand. "Nice, Bella," he said. "Very nice."

"What's nice?"

"Who, not what. Paul Bunyan."

"Oh, you mean David."

"Is that his name? Bad casting. He should be Goliath. I take it he's the new light of your life?"

Bella slanted a cut-that-out look at Chuck. "Not in the least. He's my tenant."

"That makes it convenient, doesn't it," he said, one eyebrow raised suggestively. "No one has to drive home afterward."

Bella couldn't keep from laughing. "You're impossible, Chuck. And you always were the nosiest man."

"Thank heaven you've finally given me something to be nosy about."

Still chuckling, Bella felt several pairs of eyes regarding her with knowing expressions as she returned to Mrs. Huston with apologies for keeping her waiting. But the inquisition wasn't over yet.

"I thought you said you didn't date," the older woman said as Bella sat down and resumed working on her cuticles.

"I don't."

"Then who was that?"

"He's a visitor, from my husband's family. That's all."

"Nonsense." Mrs. Huston waved away Bella's explanation with her free hand. "I saw the way he looked at you."

"How did he look at me?"

"In my day, we would have said he was smitten. I'm not sure what they say now—turned on, or whatever. But he's definitely smitten. So are you, needless to say."

"I don't think—"

"He's younger than you, of course," she went on, completely ignoring Bella's interruption. "But that's all right. Young blood is good. I had a younger lover when I was nearing fifty, and it was the best thing that could have happened to me. It doesn't last, of course, but nature did make it so that older women and younger men have similar sexual appetites, so it works out rather nicely."

"I'm glad to hear it," Bella said dryly.

"Is he here for a long time? What does he do for

a living? Does he always dress like that? I think you should talk to him about cutting his hair."

Bella responded automatically to her client's barrage of questions without really paying much attention. There were a few questions of her own that needed answers. Such as, exactly why had David come to the shop? What did he want to talk to her about? What did he want from her?

Well, she thought with wry amusement, she had a pretty good idea what he wanted from her, of course. But what did she want from him?

And how much longer could she put off answering that very question?

David stood outside the kitchen window and watched Bella, telling himself that he wasn't really spying on her. He'd been invited, after all, but he didn't want to announce his presence yet. The thing was, he really liked looking at her.

Standing at the kitchen's center island, its countertop made of a light-colored butcher block, she glanced at a page in an ancient black and white school notebook that was propped up against a glass canister of dried pasta. Then she measured flour into a sifter, totally unaware of his presence in the night's shadows. She wore her hair in a high ponytail, but several dark strands had escaped and hung down around her cheeks and neck. Her bright pink T-shirt was tucked into navy jeans, and she had a blue and white print apron tied around her waist.

Bella had a true hourglass figure, the kind immortalized by painters a century ago. Her full, curvaceous body was the very antithesis of the anorexic currently in vogue, and David closed his eyes for a moment to give thanks that there were still women out there like Bella, with enough flesh to give a man something to hold on to. And more than anything, he wanted to hold her.

When he tapped on the window, she looked up, startled. Then she gave him a welcoming smile and crossed over to open the back door. The startled look reappeared on her face when he came in.

"You cut your hair," she said wonderingly. "And shaved your beard. And you're dressed. I mean, in regular clothes. I mean . . . Oh, you know what I mean."

"I think I get the gist of it," he said dryly. "You're trying to say I look a little different."

"Quite different."

He looked down at the V-neck cotton sweater and clean, fairly new jeans he was wearing. He had made an effort to dress for Bella as though they had a real, old-fashioned date. Feeling around his hairless chin with his hand, he said, "After I saw you today, I went to a barber and had them take it all off. It sure feels good."

"Let me." Bella reached up and stroked his smooth cheek with her fingertips. He responded to her touch with a quick indrawn breath. She froze as she seemed to realize that what had begun as a casual gesture had sent a bolt of electricity through both of them. "You're right. It is smooth," she said, dropping her hand to her side.

"Do you like it?" David wished that hadn't come out, but he waited as she studied him, her gaze roving all over his face and hair.

Finally, she said, "You look . . ."

He held his breath, uncomfortable with how nervous he felt.

" . . . completely different."

"I think that's been established. Good different or bad different?"

"Oh, good, definitely good."

He let out a relieved sigh. "That's all right, then."

"I mean," she went on, "you can actually see your face. You have a very—"

Again she paused and searched for the word. He wished she would stop doing that. "Very what?"

"Handsome face. I don't think I quite realized how handsome you are."

"Really?" He felt absurdly pleased with her compliment. When he looked in the mirror in the mornings, David saw a face that was certainly agreeable, but no more than ordinary. Still, if Bella wanted to think him handsome, hell, he'd let her think whatever she wanted. "Thanks."

Again, as though she had no control over her own body's movements, she reached up and brushed a couple of red-gold strands off his forehead. Then she pulled back as though she had caught her hand in a fire. "I'm sorry."

"What for?"

"Fussing over you, I guess." As she turned away and walked into the kitchen, he realized that all this time they had been standing in an open doorway. "Come on in," she said. "I'm baking."

As he closed the door behind him, he became aware of the smell, a wonderful aroma that brought back memories of Sundays at his grandparents' house. They'd died when he was quite young, but still he remembered the smell as if it were yesterday. "Almond cookies," he said. "*Mandelbrot.*"

She nodded. "I'm in the mood. Rosh Hashanah is next week, and I always celebrate the new year by getting out the old recipes and baking up a storm. Mandelbrot and strudel and honey cookies. Dozens and dozens of them."

A buzzer went off and, reaching for a pair of pot holders, Bella took out two trays of the almond-filled logs from the oven. She set them down on the top of the stove to cool before slicing them into individual cookies.

David noticed several wicker baskets filled with

baked goods. "What do you do with all of it?" he asked.

"I bring a lot of them into the shop. I've spoiled them all—the customers and the manicurists. They've come to expect me to bake for them. I also sell them downstairs in the gift shop, to go with espresso. I kind of like doing it, especially now that the boys are gone."

At the mention of her absent sons, a wistful look crossed her face, and he wanted to put his arms around her and hug the sadness away. Instead, he leaned against the adjacent counter and crossed his arms over his chest. "When did you see them last?"

She stirred a batch of dough in a large glass bowl as she answered him. "It's been a month since they left for school. They're in their second year. Alex is in the dorm at Santa Cruz, but Sam is sharing an apartment in Berkeley this semester." Frowning with worry, she added, "I'm not sure it's the best thing for him, but he was pretty insistent."

"I'm sure he'll be fine," David said. "Will they be coming home for the new year?"

She shook her head. "They can't spare the time. I've been invited to come up and bring lots of cookies, however, so they're not avoiding me, at least."

"Will you go?"

"If this new manicurist works out tomorrow, yes."

He watched as she shaped the dough into individual logs and placed them on cookie sheets. She opened the oven door and put them in, setting the timer. "Your sons are lucky to have someone who cares about them the way you do," he said.

She looked up at him, surprised. "I'm their mother, for heaven's sake."

"Not all mothers feel the way you do."

"Oh," she said, "didn't you—? I'm sorry, it's probably none of my business."

"Didn't I what? It's all right, you can ask me anything you'd like."

She wiped her hands on her apron and leaned against the wooden edge of the counter. "Didn't you feel loved by your mother?"

Her question took him by surprise, and he thought about it for a moment. "I guess I did. Sure. It's just that"—he'd never talked about this with anyone and he wasn't certain how to say the words—"I used to think I was some sort of experiment to both of them. You know, let's have a kid and see how it feels. But there was no end to the experiment. I mean, I was born and then I was there all the time. I don't think my mother knew what to do with me."

The soft compassion in Bella's warm brown eyes made David swallow, self-conscious now and not at all happy with the direction of their conversation. He gave her a humorless half-smile. "Don't look at me that way, please."

Her eyes widened. "How am I looking at you?"

"Like I'm one of the hundred neediest cases," he replied with a touch of sarcasm. "I don't need you to feel sorry for me."

"I don't feel sorry for you."

"No?"

"No," she said firmly, clasping her hands in front of her. "What I feel is your pain. I can't help it, it's just the way I am. It's as if there's a connection between me and certain people. When they're sad, I'm sad. When they're happy, so am I. We"—she pointed to him and then herself—"you and I, we have that connection, and so I feel it when you're in pain."

"I'm not in pain."

"Well, of course you are, David. All of us are. All of us have things in our lives that didn't work out—disappointments, sorrows, losses. We wouldn't be human otherwise. It's just that—" She sighed. "You're not going to like this."

He could feel his jaw tense. "Go on."

"I was going to say that you expend so much effort not to feel your pain." Putting her hands out in a gesture of helplessness, she said, "But I do, David, I feel it. And I hurt for you."

He went still. With Bella's quiet words, an emotion flooded through him that he could not name. He stared at her, aware of a soft fluttering in his chest and the way his breath was speeding up. In the overhead light of the kitchen, her eyes seemed to shimmer. With tears? Tears for him?

He could see two smudges of flour, one on her cheek, the other on her chin. Her skin was flushed from the constant oven heat; wisps of ebony hair framed her face, some strands sticking to her full, high cheekbones. He thought it was the most beautiful face he had ever seen, would ever see. He knew that in the short time he had known her he had let her see more of what made him tick than anyone had ever seen, and—unbelievably—the world hadn't crashed down around him.

He had to connect with her, to close the distance between their bodies. What he really wanted to do was drown in her. At the very least, he had to touch her.

Bella could feel the edge of the counter pressing against the small of her back as David came toward her, his face transmitting his intentions. She had no desire to fight him. Two steps brought him to her and, placing his large hands on either side of her face, he brought his mouth down to hers.

Expelling a soft sigh, she trembled at his touch, at the feel of his firm, full mouth on hers. His kiss was unbearably gentle, yet behind it she could sense the power of his need for her, and the effort it was costing him to hold back.

Leaning her elbows on the wooden surface behind her, she arched toward him, savoring the feel of his mouth as he nibbled at her lips, then let him angle her head to grant him access to all of her face—her forehead, her eyebrows, the closed, heavy lids of her eyes. His smell surrounded her, that outdoors, masculine scent that he brought with him, mixed tonight with a subtle lime aftershave. She loved what his teasing mouth was doing to her skin, the way it felt alive and cherished for the first time in a long, long time.

But still, she couldn't bring herself to put her arms around him and mold herself to his strong body, the way she wanted to. Somehow, if she stayed like this, willing yet passive, she was still safe.

David withdrew his caressing mouth, although he continued to cup her face in his hands. "Bella," he said quietly.

She opened her eyes and gazed up at him. "Your glasses are steamed up."

His mouth curved upward. "You're right."

Removing them, he placed them next to the mixing bowl behind her. Then he gripped the edge of the counter on either side of her, not touching her, but effectively imprisoning her with his arms. Looking at her now, without the barrier of the lenses, his eyes glittered with a strange green intensity that bored deep into her soul. Silently, he asked her a question, but she couldn't bring herself to answer it.

"I don't suppose you'd like a cookie?" she said.

He blinked and looked startled, then threw back his head and laughed. It was the first time she'd heard his laughter; it was a big, rich, deep sound to go along with the rest of him.

"You're too much," he said on a chuckle. "The old avoidance syndrome again. Change the subject by offering to feed me."

"I take it that means you don't want a cookie."

"I want you, Bella. I think you know that."

"Oh." She looked down to where the V of his sweater met the pale blond curls of his chest.

"And you want me." When she didn't answer, he said, "Come on," but not with impatience. The look on his face was amused and tender as he put a finger under her chin, raising her head so she had to meet his gaze. "You told me some truths about myself a moment ago. Let me do the same for you. Since we met, there's been a connection, you said it yourself. I don't know what it is or where it will go, but it's there, and it can't be ignored. Can it?"

Still, she couldn't answer him. She felt foolish, cowardly, terrified . . . and about to melt with wanting him.

David brought his hands up to her shoulders and began to massage them with strong, supple fingers. "What is it? Tell me."

"I'm not sure." She closed her eyes. His hands felt wonderful. "How did you know?"

"How did I know what?" he asked, bringing his

head down to her neck and nuzzling her lightly, then licking the tender area near her ear.

"That all my tension goes to my shoulders?"

"I know a lot about you, Bella," he murmured. "Let me show you."

With his mouth and tongue he traced a line from her ear along the side of her neck, to find the hollow above her clavicle. She could hear herself groan as his firm yet light strokes moved from her shoulders down over her arms. Taking her hands in his, he brought them up and placed them around his neck.

"David," she said with a sigh, unable to stop her body's response as he curved his palms around the undersides of her breasts and up over the tops, lightly massaging her sensitive skin. Slowly and expertly, his thumbs rubbed her nipples into hard, tight peaks. A tremor moved all through her, invading her bloodstream with heat and pooling almost painfully between her legs. "Oh," she said, feeling helpless at his onslaught. "Oh," she said again.

David pulled Bella to him, inhaling her sweet rose scent, along with the smells of her baking—vanilla, almond, lemon. Her breasts crushed against his chest, so he could feel the tips of her distended nipples through his sweater. "Bella," he whispered, and reached again for her mouth. This time he thrust his tongue between her lips, invading her dark, honeyeyed sweetness, telling her that he was taking over now, that she didn't have to struggle anymore.

She met his surging tongue with her own, and he felt himself drowning in sensation. The room seemed to spin, and there was a great noise, like roaring, in his ears. He felt himself moving, the floor buckling slightly beneath him. There was a crash as dishes fell and pots clanged, and subtle waves of motion took over the kitchen, motion that had nothing to do with the woman in his arms.

They were in the middle of an earthquake!

FIVE

Bella felt her heart stop as the rest of her body froze in place, probably not for more than three seconds, during which time she was trying to decide whether or not to move. David solved the problem by firmly leading her to the sturdy old kitchen table and pushing her under it. "Put your hands over your head and stay down," he said.

Wondering why he wasn't joining her, she did as he told her. "Where are you going?"

"I'm right here."

The rolling and swaying went on for about ten seconds more; it felt like ten years. Bella crouched on the floor under the table and peeked out at David, who stood at the kitchen wall with the palms of his hands placed flat against it. The look on his face was one of intense, unabashed excitement. He was enjoying this! Her heart was in her mouth, she was shaking with terror and wondering if her life was over, and he was as happy as the proverbial pig in a pile of slop.

Finally, the movement stopped. Bella waited, half expecting an aftershock or two, as was often the case. But as the moments ticked by, there was silence and steadiness; the danger seemed to have passed. "Can I come out now?" she asked in a voice that to her ear sounded faintly like a child's.

"Yes," David said, his palms and the side of his head still against the wall as though he were a private detective eavesdropping on a transgression in the next room. "Turn on the TV, okay?"

Bella flipped on the small set that was on a counter by the sink, changing channels until she got a local network affiliate. A news team engaged in the usual improvised chatter, talking about what had happened to each of them personally and the phone reports coming in to the station. It was obviously too soon to have information on where the quake had been centered or an accurate seismic reading.

Bella looked around the kitchen. Two dishes had fallen from a ledge, but there seemed to be no other damage that she could see. After she disposed of the broken pieces, she reached for the phone.

"Who are you calling?" David asked.

"The boys."

"In northern California? They wouldn't have felt this."

"Still . . ." She dialed Alex's dorm number. Since the big Loma Prieta quake in the Santa Cruz mountains in 1989, she'd never been entirely easy about his attending school there. A computer voice came on, saying that all the circuits were busy.

It all caught up to her then—the classic delayed reaction—and Bella began to tremble uncontrollably. She was extremely grateful to feel David's strong arms around her, holding her close, enveloping her with warmth. "You okay?" he asked after a while, smiling down at her.

"I always think I'll get used to it, but I never do. You feel so powerless."

He nodded. "We are powerless. There's not much you can do about the earth moving."

She snuggled against his chest, comforted by the firm, steady beat of his heart. "I wish we lived where there were hurricanes—tornadoes, even. At least there's a warning then."

"Earthquakes are nature at her most powerful. She watches us, with our tall buildings and our attempts to tame her, and she laughs."

Bella jerked her head back and glared up at him. "This is fun for you, isn't it? You're having the best time!"

"As a matter of fact, I am," he said with a barely restrained undercurrent of excitement. "Listen, if you're all right, I need to get out of here."

"Where are you going?"

"I've got an open invitation from Caltech, in case of a good-size quake, to go over there and lend a hand. I'd really like to do it."

"But that's in Pasadena."

"How far is that?"

"Miles and miles. If there's no traffic on the freeway, an hour or so."

"Then I'd better get going." Giving her one final squeeze, he let her go. "You'll be all right? Remember, if there's another one, get under something solid and put your arms over your head to protect yourself."

"But David, what about you? I mean, what if there's an aftershock while you're driving, what will you do?" She felt herself trembling again. "Remember the way the freeway buckled in San Francisco a few years ago, all those cars hanging on the edge?"

He gripped her upper arms and looked at her unflinchingly. "Bella, this is my life. I study earthquakes—I get right into the middle of them, scramble around in them, sometimes with a strong chance of getting hurt. So far I've managed to live through it. I always make the assumption that I will."

"But I'll worry."

"Don't," he said sharply.

"Okay, I won't," she snapped back.

The buzzer went off then, and Bella retrieved the cookies from the oven and set the tray on a rack. As David watched her tense movements around the kitchen, his expression softened. "Try to understand. I've been on my own for a long time. I'm not used to anyone giving a damn what I do."

"Well, I do give a damn." She threw up her hands in a gesture of helplessness. "What can I say? I'm sorry."

"So am I. And it may not be very comforting, but when it comes to my safety, I do the best I can and don't even think about the rest of it. If it's my time to go, there's not a whole hell of a lot I can do about it."

She studied him for a few moments longer, then she nodded slowly. "I see. You're right, of course. There's not a whole hell of a lot any of us can do about it. Go, then. Here, let me pack up a few cookies. Maybe you can take them to the others there?"

He laughed, the deep, rich sound filling her kitchen. "Sure," he agreed. "That would be great. I can see it now, all us scientist types with our thick glasses and messy hair and ink marks all over our lab coats, munching away, getting cookie crumbs all over the seismograph." He chuckled. "I accept, but can you do it quickly? I want to get a move on."

Bella grabbed a paper plate and emptied a bunch of honey cookies onto it, then wrapped all of it in aluminum foil. Placing the bundle in his hands, she said, "Be careful."

For a moment his expression was one of amusement laced with irritation. "I'll be careful," he said, and kissed her softly.

"Oh, David." She sighed and leaned into him.

He lifted his head away from hers. "I'm looking forward to picking up where we left off."

"Maybe nature intervened for a reason."

"You don't really mean that, do you?"

She shrugged. "Right now, I think I do."

"I look forward to proving your theory wrong. See you later."

For a long time after David left, Bella sat glued to the television set, her fingertips touching her mouth where his lips had been. Wow, she thought, using one of her son's favorite expressions, did the man ever know how to kiss. Next to him, she was a rank amateur. And it was true—she was dreadfully inexperienced. Apart from the usual teenage necking, there'd been only Jake for all those years, and David was so very different from Jake in every way, but most especially in the way he kissed. A quiver of excitement whipped through her at the thought of what it would be like making love with David. But the excitement had a generous dose of fear attached to it.

Or maybe she was still reacting to the earthquake.

On the TV they were calling it a moderate one. She watched as the reporters posed the usual questions to the scientists. One of them, an attractive if bookish-looking woman, always came on camera with her baby in tow. Poor thing, Bella thought, being woken up in the middle of the night so mama could get to the lab. This wasn't the Big One, they all said, this was either an aftershock of the last one or a foreshock of the next, or a whole new quake, or . . .

On and on they went till Bella's head hurt. She felt one aftershock, a small one that lasted a few seconds at the most. After checking the rest of the house and finding no damage, she watched TV for two hours more, paying special attention when the camera panned the room at Caltech, hoping to catch a glimpse of David in the group of experts gathered there. For one brief moment she thought she saw him in the background, but it was over too soon to tell.

Had he made it to Pasadena safely? she wondered. She sighed loudly, wishing that she didn't care about him. Now there was a new name added to her worry list of friends and relatives. Jake was gone, but her two sons topped the list; she fretted over them, over their safety, if they were eating right, if they were staying away from drugs and unsafe sex.

Sex? Her babies? She didn't want to think about it.

And now there was David—one more near and dear person to fret over.

How could he get so enthusiastic about nature?

Bella wondered. All that chaos, all that destruction. It terrified her.

On the other hand, she was pretty enthusiastic about human beings, with all their chaos and tendencies to destruction. And she had a feeling that David—if not terrified—was certainly wary of them.

The quake, which turned out to be 5.9 on the Richter scale, had been centered in the Mojave Desert, about eighty miles east from where Bella lived, and nowhere near northern California. She called her sons anyway the next morning. Both were fine. She told Alex that she might be up early next week, and he encouraged her to come, saying that he and Sam wanted to take her out to dinner for her birthday. It was agreed that Sam would come down from Berkeley to Santa Cruz so she would have less of a drive, and she would see the two boys on Monday night.

When she hung up the phone, Bella looked out the window. David's jeep wasn't in the driveway. He hadn't returned last night, and she upbraided herself for her concern. He was a grown-up, after all, and owed her nothing. Just then the phone rang.

"Bella?"

"Oh, David. You're okay."

"Of course I am. I want you to know that I'm not sure when I'll be back, maybe later tonight, maybe not even till tomorrow. We're off to explore a couple of fault lines."

"All right. And thank you for calling. I really mean it."

"Yeah, well, you seemed anxious."

"What, me?" she said with a smile. "Anxious? You must be thinking of someone else."

His chuckle made a nice sound over the telephone line. "Yeah, I must be. See you."

"Oh, David—" she began, but he'd already hung up. She just wanted to warn him that Kate's shower was on Sunday, and that there'd be a lot of cars in the driveway.

"What in the world is this?"

At Kate's startled question, Bella looked up from her notepad. Her blond friend, the bride-to-be, was holding up for display what looked like a limp stuffed animal, only without the stuffing.

All the other guests stared in confusion at a narrow strip of elastic attached to a piece of cloth on which was a gaily painted elephant's face. It had broad, floppy fabric ears on either side of it, and an incongruously red trunk hanging down from the center.

"Who's it from?" Bella asked. As hostess, she'd offered to write down the gifts and their donors, so that Kate could send out thank-you notes.

Kate read the writing on a small card, then looked over at Carla. "It says it's from you."

"Courtesy of my new secretary, I'm afraid," said the attractive, dark-haired lawyer, one of Kate's longtime clients. "I'm so sorry. I was in court all this week and then had to work into the night on some other cases. I didn't have time to shop. But why in the world would she pick out something like this?"

"Do you think it's some sort of hair ornament?" Hollis piped up in her musical British accent. "Or possibly—what do you call it in the States—a G-string. Now, why in heaven's name would you give a bride such an unattractive piece of lingerie?"

Dee, Kate's teenage daughter, looked at her mother and exclaimed, "Oh God, Mom, I know what it is!"

All eyes in the room turned to the red-haired and extremely red-faced girl who was now holding her hand over her mouth, shaking with embarrassed laughter. "Okay, what is it?" Kate asked.

Dee bit her lip. "It's, uh, a kind of—I mean like . . . One of the girls at school had one of those, you know, scuzzy lingerie catalogs and . . ."

Kate frowned. "Dee," she said firmly, "if you know what the thing is, tell us."

"Okay. Well, it's . . . you know, the guy puts it on, like on the wedding night, and he— I can't!"

"Yes, you can," Bella prompted.

Carla, who had taken the piece of cloth and was

examining it as if it were evidence in a trial, said in her best attorney fashion, "What we have here is indeed a man's brief, or briefs. I suppose the purpose of it is that the man, shall we say, fills up the elephant's trunk with his—"

One of the older women gasped. Another giggled.

"Although," Carla continued as she handed the gift back to Kate, "I'm not quite sure what happens then."

"When it's full, it plays music!" Dee cried out.

"It what?" Bella exclaimed.

"A march!" Dee covered her face and fell back onto the couch, shaking with laughter. "There's a tiny transistor in there and when the trunk, like, *expands,* it plays a march!"

"Oh, no!" Kate buried her face in the cloth, then realizing what she'd done, tossed it away from her like a hot potato.

Through the boisterous female laughter came the sound of chimes. Bella looked toward her front door. Was it David? He hadn't returned yet, and she'd been half listening for him since the phone call the day before. She put down her pad and rose as the chimes sounded again, more insistently this time, cutting through the ribald remarks and giggles that filled the room.

"Don't anyone say another word until I get back," Bella warned as she crossed the hardwood floors toward the front of the house. As expected, the party was going well; most of the women had known each other for years.

"David!" she said warmly, throwing open the door. "Oh, David," she said with concern.

He looked exhausted. Tired, red-rimmed eyes, two day's worth of golden bristles, stained and rumpled clothing. And even so, ruggedly, devastatingly attractive, damn him. If it had been she who hadn't slept in days, she would have looked like a refugee direct from some war-torn country.

Smiling that half-smile of his, David leaned an elbow against the door frame and looked at her through lowered lids. "Hi. You seem to be having some sort of party, so I'm sorry to bother you. I locked myself out."

"Oh, no. Come in. I'm not sure if I have an extra key."

As she started toward the interior of the house, David hung back. "Maybe I could wait here."

"Nonsense. Come on in." Bella entered the cool, high-ceilinged living room with David right behind her, and announced, "Everyone, this is my—" She turned around to look at him. "What did we decide you are?"

He shot an amused glance at her. "We haven't, yet."

Her eyes locked on those hypnotic green ones of his; for the briefest moment it felt as if they were the only two people in the room. Then she remembered all the others. Turning back to the assembled group, she said in her best gracious-lady voice, "David is staying in the guest house."

A chorus of hellos greeted him, and it seemed to dawn on David for the first time that a dozen well-dressed women were studying him with varying degrees of curiosity. He nodded. "Ladies."

"The guest house is lovely, isn't it?" Hollis said from the couch. "I spent almost a year there."

David eyed the petite young woman. "You must be Hollis. Bella's talked about you." He glanced around the rest of the room, stopping at the sight of brightly colored packages piled all over the coffee table. "I think I'm interrupting something."

"A shower for Kate," Bella said.

"A what?"

"A *bridal* shower," Kate said. "For me."

"You know"—Dee jumped up from an overstuffed chair and came over to him—"like when someone is going to get married, and the bride gets presents and stuff?"

"Oh." With his small smile he said, "Yeah, I guess I've heard about that."

"My mom's getting married. I mean, again. You know."

David lifted an eyebrow. "That's nice."

"And her boyfriend, I mean, her fiancé, he's getting a bachelor party."

"I've heard about those too."

"And David is locked out and dying to get some sleep," Bella inserted, unable to help grinning.

David continued to stand in the middle of the floor with a look on his face that said he wasn't sure he'd made the right move coming inside—an extremely tall, exhausted rooster in a yard full of clucking hens.

"He wound up hearing a lot more than he wanted, I imagine," Bella said. "Hollis—by any chance do you still have the key to the guest house?"

"You know," Hollis replied, fumbling around in her purse, "I believe I do. There!" She held up the brass object triumphantly, then removed it from the silver ring that held her others. She got up off the couch, walked over to David, and gave it to him, craning her neck upward. Hollis barely made it to five feet. "Good Lord, you're tall," she said. "But then, everyone's tall to me."

David shot a quick, exasperated look at Bella, then glanced down at Hollis. "Thanks," he said, taking the key. "Well, I guess I'll be going."

"Why don't I fix you a plate and you can join us?" Bella indicated a long trestle table filled with several different salads and baskets of bread. There were mints, nuts, a bowl of fruit, crackers, and various cheeses. "What would you like?"

David looked at the table, then at the women looking at him looking at the table, and shook his head, chuckling. "Thanks, but I need a shower and bed more than I need food." He nodded to the assembled group again. "It was nice meeting all of you," he said, then turned to Bella. "I'll talk to you later."

He strode out of the room on his impossibly long legs, seemingly oblivious of the multiple pairs of eyes watching him. At the sound of the front door closing, everyone turned to Bella for more details about him. Several of the manicurists had seen David when he'd come to the shop, and they peppered Bella with questions and sly insinuations.

Instead of acknowledging them, Bella looked to Kate for backup, suggesting brightly, "Why don't we go back to opening presents?"

"Okay," Kate announced, taking her cue. "Back to the festivities." With good-natured grumbling, the women resumed their places around the coffee table.

The grandfather clock in the hallway struck ten. Bella was seated at the kitchen table, watching an old thirties comedy on the small TV. The house was back in order, dishes washed, leftover food disposed of or in the freezer. Plants watered, a note left for the water delivery man. All was ready for the trip in the morning. She thought briefly of Brownie, the mutt that had been the fifth member of the family for years, and how she'd had to put him in a kennel. Going away used to be so difficult, so many arrangements to make.

Now, when she wanted to go away, there was no one she had to report to, no child or pet to make arrangements for.

As the joke went, that was the good news and the bad.

Turning her attention back to the movie, she jumped when David tapped on the windowpane. She got up and opened the door to him, suppressing the urge to run into his arms. Part of her still thought what had passed between them on Friday night— before the earthquake—was a mistake, even as the rest of her realized that all her senses sharpened with desire at the very sight of him. "Hi," she said cheerfully. "Come on in."

Now that David was rested and showered and almost back to normal, he had thought he would walk into the kitchen and pick up where he and Bella had left off. But something in her attitude, in the way she greeted him with generic friendliness and then looked down at the floor, told him that it wouldn't be quite that easy. "So, did everything go well today?"

"Yes. Everyone agreed it was a smashing success. Kate has enough lingerie for several husbands. Grab a chair," she said, seating herself once again at the table.

He took the same corner of the booth as he had several times before. Here in Bella's kitchen, sitting with her at this table—the whole thing was starting to feel comfortable. Familiar. A word with the same root as . . . family.

Funny, he'd missed this sense of hominess his entire life. Could you miss something you'd never had? he wondered.

"So," Bella said. "Would you—? Nope, I'm not going to do that."

"Do what?"

"Offer you food. You'll say I'm avoiding something."

"Are you?"

"No."

He shrugged easily. "Okay then."

She traced a pattern over the wood grain, then looked up at him again. "But are you—? I mean, do you—?"

He smiled. "Do I what?" He was on to her. Yes, she was avoiding dealing with their physical relationship, but she was also fretting over whether he'd eaten enough in his two days in the trenches. As a matter of fact, he'd been fed a lot and often. But none of it had tasted as if Bella had made it.

She crossed her arms over her chest. "I am not going to say a thing about food. Not a thing."

"All right." He sprawled easily in his chair, stretching his legs out in front of him.

"And you can stop sitting there with that smug smile on your face. In fact, you can leave. I have to get up early in the morning."

"Is it your day to attack the weeds again?"

"No, Mr. Superior. I'm leaving."

He felt the smile wipe itself off his face with amazing rapidity. "Where are you going?"

"To see my sons. I told you I might."

"Then you found a new manicurist."

"No, but Jodie—she used to work for me—just got divorced and wants to come back temporarily while she goes to computer school. So, everything is all set."

"I see," he said. "Are you driving?"

"Yes."

"In the Volvo?"

"It's my car."

"Why don't I go with you?"

"What?"

It had just popped out, but as long as it had . . . "I guess I'm inviting myself along. In the jeep, though. I think it's more trustworthy. And better for the terrain."

"The terrain is Highway 101—it's paved."

"I was thinking of avoiding the main roads, take a little longer to get there. We could follow the San Andreas fault line. It runs parallel to the coast, but more inland. We can bypass the fast food restaurants and gas stations and see some scenery. And we could go through Parkfield," he added, his enthusiasm for the trip growing even more at the thought; he'd wanted to visit Parkfield since coming to California. "How about it?"

"I don't know what to say."

He fought down a wave of disappointment. He'd been guilty of fantasizing Bella's reaction, which was supposed to go something along the lines of: Of course I want you to come along. I can't wait to be alone with you.

Straightening up, he leaned his elbows on the table. "I'm sorry, Bella. I'm being kind of forward here, inviting myself along. Maybe you need some time alone, which I understand, believe me. I get like that too."

"Oh, no. I don't want to be alone. I mean—well, what about the dig in Santa Monica? I thought you said you'd be working there full-time."

"This last quake messed around with our trench. We won't get back to it until Wednesday. So, I could join you. Drive up Monday, come back Tuesday."

"I guess not, then. I was thinking of taking an extra day and not coming back till Wednesday night."

He did a quick calculation in his head and made it come out the way he wanted it to. "No problem. I can take an extra day too."

David's last words hung in the air while Bella pondered her next response. After the rapid-fire conversation, the quiet felt strange. Outside, a cricket chirped. From the small TV came the sound of a man and woman coyly bantering. A clock ticked, the refrigerator hummed. Bella folded her hands on the table, searching David's face, not quite ready to commit herself to anything. "What is Parkfield?" she asked.

"You've probably read about it. It's that little town where they have a quake every twenty-two years on the nose."

"When was the last one?"

"A year ago."

"Whew. That's a relief."

They smiled at each other, the subtle tension in the room easing up a bit.

"So," she said, "this trip will be like research for you."

"A little. But not much. A couple of hours, maybe." He paused, then reached his hand over to where hers were still folded, like a good little girl, and stroked one long finger along the skin of her knuckles, then down to her wrist and back again. She trembled at his touch. "The rest of the time," he said softly, "I intend devoting to you."

Bella sucked in a breath, fully understanding what David was saying. This was no casual, friends-only trip. If she agreed to his company, she was agreeing to intimacy, giving the okay to their making love.

But she wasn't that kind of woman; she didn't engage in casual sex.

Come off it, she told herself. There was nothing casual about what she felt for David, and she knew it. Besides, her body had needs, needs she'd been ignoring for too long. Her two best friends, Kate and Hollis, would tell her to finally take some pleasure for herself, and if the consequences of that were difficult or painful, well, she would face them then. Right now the thought of two nights in David's arms was more than enticing. It was impossible to resist.

"Bella," David said, interrupting her thoughts, "if you don't want me to go . . ."

She met his gaze. His face was impassive, but she could sense the vulnerability below the surface. "Oh, no, David. The fact is, I would like you to come along. I would like it very much."

She felt rather than saw the tension leave his body. He gave her one of his unguarded, joyful grins. "Well, all right. What time to do we leave?"

SIX

Carefully following a United States Geological Survey map and a detailed road guide, David steered the jeep along back roads through small towns that Bella knew existed but had never traveled before. Always, in their trips up north toward the San Francisco Bay area, the Stein family had taken the freeway, pausing at the usual tourist stopping-off places—Ventura Harbor, Hearst Castle, Andersen's for a bowl of the restaurant's famous split pea soup. But this route, through mountains and valleys, through farmland and quiet little villages was as far away from her freeway life-style as she could get.

So much brown, Bella thought, great brown hills the color of discarded teddy bears. Muted, yet strangely majestic. Live oaks, with their grayish-green leaves and gnarled branches. Golden-wheat-colored bushes and scrub brush. Parched, arid. How different this was from the manicured lawns and carefully trimmed trees of southern California; different . . . and beautiful.

The drive was relaxing; no, Bella corrected herself, *she* was relaxed, probably because she had stopped fighting her attraction to David. When she thought about what the night would bring, she felt both excited and a little shy. Still, the battle was over. She admitted and accepted that fact; she spent equal time looking at the scenery and at the profile of the man driving them through it.

David's nose, like the rest of him, was long, with full nostrils and a generous bump in the middle. It was a very masculine nose, one that some who were vain might have had straightened. From what Bella could tell, David didn't seem to have any vanity at all.

He was dressed in very old jeans with what looked like some very old rips at the knees. He'd rolled up the sleeves of his blue cambric shirt so that she could fully admire the pale gold hair that sprinkled his sleekly muscled arms, could study his long fingers draped easily over the steering wheel as he drove.

He'd shaved again, and she wished he hadn't. Part of her initial fantasy about David had been to see what it felt like to have that full red-gold beard against her skin—did it tickle? Did it hurt? She'd never experienced a sensation like that before. In fact, she had a feeling that with David there were going to be a lot of experiences—and sensations—that were new, to her anyway.

She suppressed the urge to giggle, feeling a little foolish at the direction of her thoughts, which sounded to her as if she'd eavesdropped on some love-struck teenager. But then she forgave herself. It was time, after all, to be good to herself, to allow herself to take some joy out of life. A birthday present, at the very least.

They stopped for breakfast at a fifties-style coffee shop in one of the little towns and had eggs, hash browns, crispy toast, and fresh orange juice, then continued on their roundabout journey to see her sons. In the jeep, they chatted easily about his work and hers, and she wondered aloud what the Jewish New Year meant to him.

"Not much," David said. "I had hardly any religious training or observance. After my grandparents died, we paid no attention at all when it came around."

"Not us," Bella said. "I remember it as family time—big dinners and lots of cousins, going to temple and hearing all those beautiful songs. I guess I take it kind of seriously. I mean, I really do meditate on what I did wrong the past year and try to think of what I can do better for the next. The concept of renewal is a wonderful one. You get to start over, to have another chance."

"It is a good concept. I sometimes regret that

I wasn't raised with more awareness of my heritage."

"It's never too late to start."

He shot her a wry smile. "Proselytizing, are you?"

"Just commenting," she answered innocently.

"It's probably wasted on me. Somehow I don't think of you as having any great sins to atone for."

"Usually they're little ones—an unkind word here and there, fudging on my tax return. It's the starting-over part that I think of most. Especially this year."

"Why?"

She thought about it for a moment, then answered, "Jake, I think. I've come through some kind of passage in the mourning process. I'm—oh, I don't know—ready to live again."

She didn't add that the day when she'd driven up her driveway and David had been waiting there was very much part of her feeling of renewal.

"I'd been thinking of myself as used up," she went on, "unnecessary."

"That's hard to believe. You're so filled with life."

"Still, when Jake died, it felt like part of me stopped living. I was in a widow's group for a while, and most of the women felt the same way I did."

"I envy you that kind of deep feeling," he said slowly. "I guess I've never let myself care enough about anyone to mourn them when they were gone."

Again she glanced over at him; he'd said the words in that detached style of his, but his mouth was set in a stern line. How empty David's life had been, she thought. And devoid of meaning. But maybe she was judging him by her own standards; maybe he was perfectly fine the way he was. Maybe, as he said, he was incapable of deep feelings.

A chill came over her at the thought. She had to keep that in mind: David wasn't the kind of man to stick around and form deep attachments. When it was time for him to go, he would walk away and never look back.

In the early afternoon they came over a rise; below them, nestled between rolling hills and grassy meadows, was a tiny collection of farms and ranches. Bella noted how sparsely populated the area was—no houses that she could observe, not even a real town, except for something that looked like a half-block of stores.

"Parkfield," David said as they made their way down into the valley.

"But it's so small."

"Population under two hundred, not counting all the seismologists who wander around most of the time."

"Why is it so popular?"

"It straddles a big chunk of the San Andreas fault

at a point where two plates meet. Do you know what I mean by plates?"

"Not the dinner kind, obviously."

"Obviously," he said with a smile. "The whole world is made up of plates—these huge land masses going in different directions. Parkfield is right over one plate that moves constantly, and another which doesn't. That builds up friction. The result is a periodic quake—about every twenty-two years, give or take five years."

"But it looks so tiny, so peaceful."

They drove by cattle munching on grass; a soft breeze caught the top of a tall pine tree, making it sway.

"Above ground it is," David said. "But there are more seismic instruments here than in any other spot on the planet. They've sunk strain gauges way down into the earth, up to a thousand feet, and there are creep meters that measure rock movements. You can't sneeze in Parkfield without someone calibrating it."

"What are they hoping to find?"

"There's a theory that by studying this particular area, it will be possible to learn how to predict earthquakes minutes or even days before."

"That would be nice, wouldn't it?"

"I'm not sure that will ever be possible, but it's an interesting theory."

They drove on into the valley, passing huge oak and eucalyptus trees with gracefully draping branches.

David turned off onto a side road, then steered the jeep along a flat dirt path that was a saddle between two rolling hills. He pulled to a stop at what looked to Bella like several slabs of granite rock jutting out over a small cliff. A few other vehicles were also parked there—a small truck, a van and two other four-wheel-drives. The immediate terrain was composed of pebbles, pines, and chaparral.

They got out of the car. Toward the cliff's edge, David hunkered down and, scraping aside some dried pine needles, he scooped up a handful of the soil beneath. It had the color and consistency of coarsely ground eggshells. He looked up at Bella, smiling. "This little hill we're on was probably created in one earthquake, and not too long ago, sometime in the last century."

"Seriously?" She crouched down next to him and looked at the soil in his hand.

He rubbed his thumb over it. "This is granite rock that got pulverized by the edges of the plates grinding away at each other. In the quake of 1857, or maybe even the one in eighty-one, this stuff was heaved up out of the fault and deposited right here, most probably in the space of a couple of minutes. *Voilà!*" he said with a flourish. "A hill is born."

"Absolutely amazing. You're opening up a new world to me, you know. I've never thought of earthquakes as anything except something to be feared, especially living in California."

"Earthquakes are what shaped California. If it weren't for the faults coming through here, the whole state would be a deserty sort of Kansas. Completely flat. Earthquakes formed all the mountains, and definitely made the state a more interesting place."

"Interesting," she observed wryly, "if it weren't for the danger."

"That's the fun part," David said, and she knew he meant it. Rising, he looked over toward an outcropping in front of which was a wooden barricade with the words KEEP OUT written across it. "I need to check this out. Why don't you sit here for a few minutes. I'll be right back."

She nodded, remaining where she was, looking out toward the faraway mountains and thinking that she was happier than she'd been for a very long time. She'd never been an outdoor person—gardening was the extent of her contact with nature—but there was something about this setting, and David's presence in it, that made her feel like part of a greater whole.

After a while she got up and wandered over toward a small copse of cottonwood trees, their shiny green leaves offering shade on this hot September day. She leaned down over a narrow stream, barely trickling at this time of year, and managed to scoop up enough water to wipe around her face.

What was David doing? she wondered. Walking over to the Keep Out sign, she went around it as he had. She picked her way along a huge boulder, then turned a corner to see him in the distance, forty or fifty yards away. He had obviously leapt across a small chasm that with her shorter legs and less-athletic nature she wouldn't dare attempt. So she sat down on a shaded slab of rock and watched him.

He was perched at the edge of a large trench, his legs dangling over the side, and talking to someone she couldn't see. With no trees nearby to offer shelter, he was in full sunlight, and his shirt lay on the ground next to him. Nodding to whomever he was talking to, he lifted an arm to wipe sweat off his face, then reached into the back pocket of his jeans. He removed a brightly colored bandanna and wrapped it around his forehead, Indian fashion.

Gone were all vestiges of the clinical scientist; in its place was a lean yet muscular, bare-chested warrior, his skin golden and shiny, his flame-colored hair glinting in the sunlight. He was a magnificent sight; Bella felt her breathing rate escalate as she stared at him shamelessly, comforted by the fact that he didn't know she was there.

After a while, balancing himself on his hands, David lowered himself into the trench. Now that he was out of sight, Bella allowed herself to lean back against the boulder and stare off again at the distant mountains, trying to picture them being formed by molten rocks spewing up from the planet's interior. A warm breeze ruffled her hair which she wore loose today. Closing her eyes, she could smell the scent of the eucalyptus floating on the breeze. Nearby, a bird twittered and another answered. A bee buzzed in the distance. . . .

"Hey there, sleeping beauty. Wake up."

Bella opened her eyes abruptly to see David standing over her. She'd been dreaming about him, but her dreams couldn't compare with him in the flesh. His hair was tousled and there were beads of sweat running down the sides of his face that his soaked bandanna hadn't been able to catch. His shirtless chest glowed with healthy male perspiration as he stood, one hip cocked, a thumb in the waistband of his jeans, his shirt tossed over his shoulder. He exuded masculinity in a way that made her feel weak with wanting him; the expression on his face as he stared down at her was enough to make her insides turn to pure Jell-O.

"How long have I been asleep?" she asked, shading her eyes as she looked up at him.

He crouched down next to her and reached out with his long fingers to stroke her hair. "About an hour. God, you're beautiful."

She was about to say that she wasn't, but she was constrained by a look of hunger in his eyes that struck her dumb. She moistened her suddenly dry lips. He offered his hand and she allowed herself to be pulled up against him, their bodies touching for the briefest moment. It was enough to titillate her own sensual appetite and start her heart pounding.

She looked at her feet, embarrassed by the strength of her reaction to him. "David, I don't think—"

"Don't worry," he said with a smile in his voice. "I'm not going to attack you, not here and now anyway. Come on." He took her hand and led her toward the car.

"Where to?"

"Someplace with a flat ground and some shade. I'm really looking forward to that picnic you brought."

They found a large oak tree in the corner of a meadow, and Bella suggested David stretch out under it while she organized the picnic. He'd done all the driving, she said—it was only right that she do all the feeding.

"As I'm helpless in the kitchen," he said, sinking onto the ground and leaning back against a thick tree trunk, "I bow to your greater expertise."

"Have you ever wanted to cook?" She'd brought along an old army blanket and she knelt in the middle of it, smoothing out the corners.

"Never. I don't have a domestic bone in my body. You should see my apartment. I rent it furnished, and it looks it."

"I just realized I have no idea where you live."

Closing his eyes, he folded his hands over his

stomach. "The world is my home, as they say. But I get my mail in Albuquerque."

"Your parents live in Cambridge, don't they?" she asked, reaching into a huge wicker basket and setting out thick turkey sandwiches, pickles, and homemade potato salad.

"Which is why I live in Albuquerque. We don't see each other very much."

"You're estranged?"

"That's too extreme. We're indifferent."

She stopped in the middle of unwrapping the sandwiches. Sitting back on her heels, she studied him for a moment before asking, "What happened to you, David? Why are you like that?"

David opened his eyes, puzzled, but arrested by the tone of Bella's voice. "Why am I like what?"

"Pretending that you don't care, purposely not setting down roots, keeping yourself apart."

He started to tell her that she was reading him wrong, that it wasn't pretense. But that wouldn't be the truth, and he knew it was somehow important to try to be truthful with Bella. Still, he didn't quite know how to answer her.

She removed more condiments and paper goods from the picnic basket. "I guess you'd rather not talk about it," she said.

"I don't mind talking about it, Bella." He was amazed that it was so. "It's just that I'm not sure I have any answers. I was a funny kind of kid, not ha-ha funny, but weird, I guess. I spent most of my childhood feeling as if I'd been dropped into my family from another planet, and they seemed to agree. We never talked. They never got a handle on what to do with me. I was always marching to a different drummer."

It was odd, David thought, thinking back to when he was a kid. He rarely indulged in introspection. But today was unlike other days.

"Besides," he went on, "they weren't around much. They're both well thought of in their fields and they traveled a lot, doing research, guest lectures, stuff like that. Still do. I got left a lot with baby-sitters, and most of them didn't know what to do with me either. I had a mind of my own and I guess I was pretty obnoxious."

"Were you?"

Was he? The memories came flooding back. Brisk, silent dinners—his mother, his father, and him, the three of them with little or nothing to say to each other. Hibernating in his room for hours on end, with his books and his rock collection. When he was old enough, long, solitary walks through the Boston streets after school and on weekends; science camps in the summers. Anything to stay away from them, from the apartment they called home, from the knowledge that he was never lonelier than when he was with his parents.

He tried to shake off a sudden piercing sadness for the little boy he once was, but it wasn't an easy thing to do. He looked over at Bella. She was watching him with that way she had of intense, concentrated listening; it was so totally supportive, it made him feel that what he said was really interesting.

"It's funny," he mused, "I don't ever remember being held. Or told I was special. Or even that I was loved. And I guess that answers your question. If you don't have it as a child, you grow up unable to feel it. Or so they say."

This last part was said in that detached tone of voice, as if he were discussing an interesting specimen, but Bella knew David well enough by now to see that he was covering again, something he'd obviously learned to do a long time ago. She looked down at the blanket so he wouldn't see her eyes filling with tears. He seemed to have the capacity to move her unbearably, more for what he hid than what he revealed. But she didn't want him to see her crying for him; he would interpret her compassion as pity. Even so, she couldn't shake a picture that had formed in her head as he spoke—a young child holding his arms out for a hug, with no one there to pick him up.

How dare they, she thought. How dare people have children and not cherish them!

"So," David said, shrugging, "we don't talk much, my parents and I."

"I see."

"Bella?"

"Hmm?"

"Are you okay?"

"Yes. Come on and eat."

Frowning, David pushed himself away from the tree and joined her on the blanket. For several moments they each sat, cross-legged, and took bites of their sandwiches. Bella seemed distracted and distant. Probably he shouldn't have told her as much as he had. Had he sounded self-pitying? He couldn't tolerate the thought.

Setting his plate on the blanket, he lay down on his side, resting his head on his hand. "You went away. Talk to me."

She smiled bleakly, then wiped around her mouth with a napkin. "I was thinking."

"About my sad tale? Don't."

"Too late. It started me remembering my own sad tale. Children are so hungry for love, aren't they? My aunt and uncle, well, they tried, I guess, but they weren't very demonstrative. I used to adopt all kinds of animals just to have something soft to hug. I think that's why I was so drawn to Jake. He was the most affectionate man I'd ever met. And I loved his family. They welcomed me as if I were their long-lost daughter. It was so special."

"Tell me about him."

"Jake?"

She smiled tenderly, and David felt a small spurt of jealousy go through him.

"He was round and comforting," she said. "When I was afraid, he made me feel safe. He was quite a bit older than me—fifteen years. I guess he was a father figure, but we got past that, especially after he got sick."

"When was that?"

"He had the first stroke, let me see, we'd been married about ten years. He went to bed one night, cracking a joke, and woke up the next morning like an infant. He spent three months in the hospital, part of the time in a coma. He was never able to go back to work full-time again. And there we were with the huge house and huge mortgage. Anna and I had opened the new shop." She shook her head ruefully. "It was not an easy time."

"Did Jake recover?"

"Only partly. He was paralyzed on one side. He never drove again—no peripheral vision. Still, he helped me with the books and advice on running the business. And he listened when I needed to talk. We had some savings, and I worked real hard at the shop, and I thought we were going to get through it. Then he had another stroke, and a month later he was dead."

David raised up slightly, supporting himself on an elbow. "My God, I had no idea. You said Jake had been sick, so I figured a few months, maybe. But you took care of him much longer than that, for years, it sounds like. And the boys. And a business. How the hell did you do it?"

"What choice was there?" she countered simply. "You have a sick husband, you take care of him. You have children, you raise them. You have a business, you run it the best you can. There was no other option."

"If you say so."

"And it wasn't an unrelenting tragedy, or anything like that. The boys were so much fun, and such a challenge. And the shop—Anna, the other manicurists, they were like family. I cried sometimes, when it got to be too much, but there was always someone to talk to, to get a pat on the back from. Poor Jake, he was the one who suffered most. He was such a good man. I was so lucky to have him."

"And he was lucky to have you. Damned lucky."

She made a face. "Stop, you're embarrassing me. Eat."

His sudden grin startled her, but then she grinned back, shaking her head at her own folly.

"It's true, isn't it? Whenever I'm uncomfortable, I offer food. I've probably been that way all my life. Why did you have to tell me? I'm going to be self-conscious."

"Then we're even. I feel self-conscious about a couple of the things I said too."

Bella put her hand over his, and her expression

became serious. "Don't be. Nothing you said was anything other than . . . terribly human. It made me understand you better, and I'm glad."

They smiled, almost shyly, at each other. Brimming with an emotion that was hard to name, Bella felt closer to David than she ever had; she could feel laughter bubbling up inside her at that magical sense of connectedness they had shared. Something important had occurred between them, although what, she couldn't say.

She let out a huge breath. "So, how about dessert? This is not about my being uncomfortable, I promise. I don't want all this food to go to waste."

"What do you have?"

"Iced tea and cookies."

"Bring them on."

David finished off his sandwich and dug into the cookies while Bella sat, resting her elbows on her knees and grinning happily. She loved to watch him eat. He did it with enormous enthusiasm. And besides, he really did need to put on a few pounds. She wished there were an operation that would take a few from her hips and distribute them evenly over David's body.

Munching on his fifth cookie, David lay back on the blanket and looked up at the sky through the shimmering oak leaves. "This is as close to nirvana as I can imagine."

He reached over for her hand, pulling her down

so that she was lying next to him on the blanket. Closing her eyes as he rubbed his thumb back and forth over her knuckles, she sighed audibly. Nirvana indeed.

"Did I tell you your cookies were the hit of Caltech?" he asked.

"No, you didn't." Opening her eyes, she looked over at him with a delighted smile. "That means a lot."

"You're something, Bella, you really are." He brought her hand up to his face and rubbed her palm over his cheek; she could feel the new stubble growing there. "You bake, you garden, you quilt. I didn't know your kind existed anymore."

"Awful, isn't it? I try to hide it sometimes, but I'm terribly old-fashioned in a lot of ways. Guess I'm ready for the old folks' home."

"Hardly that," David said, turning on his side and pulling her to him. Cupping her face in his hands, he kissed her long and thoroughly, till she heard someone moan softly, and knew it was she.

"David," she whispered.

"I love the way you say my name," he murmured, then kissed her again, angling her face so that he could taste more of her. How could one pair of lips taste so sweet? he wondered.

Bella pressed against him, trying to get as close as she could, and he seemed to sense that, because he shifted their bodies so that he was on top of her. She was aware of his growing arousal pressing against her legs, and it filled her with a sense of her own power—it was exhilarating to be wanted like this. A surge of joy flooded her. Raking her fingers through his hair, she opened her mouth wider to receive his kiss with an eagerness she thought she had left behind years ago.

"Mmm."

The sound did not come from David. Nor from her. It was behind her.

They were not alone.

Bella froze. Pushing herself away from him, she turned so she could see over her shoulder. Standing not ten feet from them was a brown and white cow. Next to the cow was a towheaded young boy, eight or nine years old. He stared at them, his sweet young face completely expressionless.

Bella looked at David and he looked at her, then they both burst out laughing. The solemn-faced child continued to stare at them. Sitting up, Bella waved one hand in the air and said, "Hi."

He didn't reply, but the cow mooed again and ambled off toward the road. With a final grave look, the boy followed. Bella watched him walk away, a fond smile on her face.

David put his arms around her and pulled her back down, tucking her head under his chin. "Don't you dare tell me that was nature interfering again," he said.

"Okay, I won't. But you have to admit we have the oddest luck in this area. An earthquake, a cow. What's next?"

"I know what I'd like to be next. But I think it can wait till we find a little more privacy."

She was silent for a while. Her finger traced a pattern on his bare chest above where his shirt was buttoned. He could tell that she was trying to think of a way to say something.

"The direct way is usually the best," he prompted her.

After a deep sigh, she said, "Okay, here goes. I—uh—I'm not real experienced in this"—she waved her hand vaguely—"man and woman nineties-style thing. I mean, I want to make sure . . . Oh, David."

"You want to know if I have protection?"

She nodded. "Yes." She looked up at him, her expression both anxious and chagrined. "Do you?"

"You don't have to worry, Bella."

"David?"

"Hmm?"

"Thank you."

She was unusually quiet as they drove along. "We okay, Bella?" he asked.

"Sure. It's just that I don't do this very often." She laughed. "At all, actually."

"Do what?"

"Kiss. Go away with a man. Talk about things like protection."

"Surely you've dated some since Jake died."

"No." She angled her body so she was facing him. "And Jake was the first, David. Also the only man I've ever known. I feel kind of silly, at my age, to be so unworldly. Do you mind?"

He caught her hand in his and kissed the palm. "Not in the least. In fact, it's quite a turn-on."

"Is it? Good . . . I guess."

For the next few minutes she watched the scenery. Then she said, "I missed the sixties—I was too young. But I wonder if I'd have fit in then. It didn't seem very . . . personal, somehow. You could sleep with anyone you wanted to, and the pill and penicillin took care of everything. Nowadays, you have to choose your partner with such care. It takes away from the romance, doesn't it? There are so many things you have to worry about."

"If you're concerned about me, I give blood at the Red Cross every six months, and I'm free of disease."

"Well, so am I, of course. I mean, there's only been Jake. But there's the chance of pregnancy, David. It wouldn't be the smartest thing to have happen."

"There's no chance of that."

"There's always that chance."

"Not with me. After my marriage ended, I got to

thinking, and I decided I really didn't want to bring children into this world. In fact, I couldn't imagine why anyone would want kids. So, I took care that I never would."

"You mean—?"

He nodded. "Yes. I had a vasectomy."

Bella received David's news with outward calm, but inside her feelings were churning. How final that act was—how desolate David's childhood must have been to bring him to that. Oh, David, she wanted to say, how could you?

Searing disappointment followed, and she realized that somewhere deep inside, she would have liked to have had his child. If the timing were different, of course—if she were younger, if they had met at another stage in each other's lives—she would at least have entertained the fantasy that together they would create a new life.

But even a fantasy was out of the question, and that realization hurt, and hurt deeply. She was being unreasonable, she supposed, to be upset with a man for punching holes in a private fantasy. But in fact, she was in love with that man.

The realization struck her at that moment. She loved him. She had warned herself not to care too much, but it was too late.

Oh, Bella, she admonished herself. *What have you done?*

SEVEN

David smiled as he perused the wall in Alex's dorm room. A *Rolling Stone* cover of David Letterman, posters of The Black Crowes, Pearl Jam, Cindy Crawford, and the Beatles, a blow-up of a Gary Larson cartoon, a Los Angeles Kings pennant, and several Monet prints of gardens and lilies, with signs preaching ecological awareness and Amnesty International. An eclectic kid, for sure, he thought. On a bookcase in the corner was a framed portrait of Bella, two young boys, and a man who was undoubtedly Jake.

Bella had called her late husband paternal, and that would describe the man in the photo, balding and with a face that was more good-natured than handsome. David tried to recall if he'd seen pictures of Jake in Bella's house, then remembered that the only room he'd been in for any length of time was the kitchen. Up till now, he was, he supposed, the back-door man. The tenant.

Not any longer. Not after tonight. His blood had been heating up in expectation all day. Several times, in fact, he had wanted to grab Bella and gratify their mutual thirst, but the timing—that damned timing again—hadn't been right. Soon, though, she would be in his arms and he would be buried deeply in her soft body, obliterating the world and all its reality.

But first there was dinner with her sons.

Alex was a nice kid, warm like his mother and easy to talk to. He definitely favored Bella both in temperament and looks. He was tallish, with her ebony hair and brown eyes. There was a gentleness about him that in no way took away from his masculinity.

Alex allowed Bella to hug him without complaint, even hugging her back. The boy was courteous to David, shaking his hand when she introduced him as a distant relative of his father's. The three of them sat around and talked as they waited for Sam to arrive from Berkeley.

Bella kept her distance from David; it was obvious to him that she wanted no hint of anything other than family ties given to the boys. There were no quick touches, no intimate looks, nothing to reveal that they had kissed and more, and that later they would kiss and much more.

"David has a very interesting kind of job," Bella told Alex. "He studies earthquakes."

"Really?" Alex seemed genuinely interested, and asked him a lot of questions. They also talked about crossword puzzles and trivia games—the family had a definite predilection for the verbal. The kid was okay, David thought. Bright but not super driven.

The chemistry in the room changed the minute Sam hurried in. "I'm sorry I'm late," he said. "This guy who was supposed to give me a ride from Berkeley got hung up with his girlfriend, and so I borrowed this other guy's car, but his gas gauge is broken, and I ran out of gas and, Mom, I knew you'd be freaking out, so I hauled it getting here."

At the end of this speech he gave Bella a peck on the cheek, said hello to Alex, and seemed to notice David for the first time. "Who are you?"

As Bella made the introductions, David saw that there was a familial resemblance, but Sam and Alex were not identical twins. Sam was shorter and stockier with light brown hair. Like his brother, he had also inherited Bella's eyes, and looking at all three of them was like looking at a row of shiny brown marbles.

Sam was more hyper than Alex, also more closed up, less accessible. He shook David's hand with a glint of wariness in his eyes, and stood stiffly when Bella hugged him hello. He loved her, it was obvious, but he was less at ease with her than Alex was. It was as if he'd drawn a line between him and his mother, over which she was not to cross.

The two brothers seemed close, though, punching each other's arms and laughing at a stupid joke. Bella beamed at them both with unconditional maternal love, and for the second time that day David felt jealous. He wanted her to care about him as fiercely as she did her late husband and her two sons. How unreasonable he was being, he thought. They hadn't even slept together, and he was feeling possessive, territorial almost. It was so unlike him; hell, most of his reactions to Bella were so unlike him. He wasn't real nuts about all these . . . emotions. He'd made do without them for a long time, so long, in fact, that he'd assumed he'd make do without them forever.

So much for assumptions, he thought wryly, sitting in Alex's desk chair and watching the three of them talk and laugh. As comfortable as Alex was with his mother and her gentle fussing, that's how uncomfortable Sam was. Two opposite reactions to the same stimulus. Interesting. People were sure interesting.

"Well," Alex said, rising from his narrow dorm bed. "Let's do it. I'm hungry."

Bella looked at her watch. "Oh, I didn't realize the time. I have to change."

"But, Mom . . ." Alex said.

"We were a little late getting here," she said,

avoiding David's eyes, "and we haven't even got a motel yet."

"We can find one later," David said. "I saw plenty of vacancy signs as we drove through town."

"But I want to freshen up, to change clothes."

"Oh, Mom," Sam said, "that will take forever. You know how you are." Turning to David, he explained, "Mom used to make Dad crazy, keeping him waiting an hour while she fussed over her makeup."

"It was never more than ten minutes, so please stop exaggerating. I just thought if we're going to a nice place, I ought to—"

"Nice place?" Sam exclaimed. "Mom, neither of us can afford a nice place. I mean, Santa Cruz isn't like that."

"It's very casual," Alex added, finishing his twin's thought. "You know, jeans and T-shirts, that's all."

"I like the sound of that a lot," David piped in.

"You would." Bella looked down at her cotton culottes and light knit sweater. "You mean what I'm wearing is all right?"

"It's terrific, Mom," Alex said. "I'm starving."

"All right, I hear you. May I at least wash my face and hands?"

"Well, sure. Down the hall."

"Are the bathrooms still coed?"

"Yes."

She shuddered. Grabbing her oversize bag, she said, "Five minutes."

"It better be," Sam called after her.

Then the boys and David were alone in the room. Facing the mirror over his dresser, Alex ran a comb through his hair while Sam perched on the edge of the bed and stared at David. "So, if you're a relative, how come I've never met you?"

"Because I'm a very distant one. I met your mother for the first time last week, and I never met your dad."

"Why are you in L.A.?"

"I'm attached to a research project out of U.C.L.A."

"Are you staying with Mom?"

"Hey, Sam, cool it," Alex said. "The guy doesn't need the third degree."

"I'm staying in the guest house till the project is over, which should be in four to six weeks."

Sam's chin jutted out. "I just wanted to know, that's all."

David smiled, not at all offended by Sam's questions. "What is it exactly you want to know?"

The young man looked at him, suspicion gleaming in his eyes. "Are you sleeping with her?"

"Sam!" said Alex. "That's none of your business."

"Are you?"

"No," David answered. Which was the truth, for the moment.

"Okay," Sam said, the air in the room less chilly suddenly as his posture relaxed.

Far from feeling defensive or angry at Sam's questions, David found himself admiring the way the kid was looking out for his mother. This was one of the pluses of family life, he supposed, the way individual members took care of each other. It was all new to him, but today at least, he was a willing pupil.

When Bella returned, shaking her head at how the students could let the communal bathrooms get so messy, she found the three men discussing the merits of East Coast vs. West Coast, shooting out statistics on colleges, sports teams, and weather. The boys seemed to like David, both looking up to him and trying to establish equality at the same time.

Don't get too attached, she wanted to say. He won't be around that long.

Later on at the restaurant, she wondered if it had been a mistake inviting David along. The man made her senses quiver, that was all there was to it, and she was having a hard time devoting her attention to the boys. The four of them sat in the town's favorite pizza place, off the pier. All the waiters—both sexes—had long hair, and the whole place was a psychedelic-era re-creation, from Led Zeppelin posters on the walls to Janis Joplin and Jimi Hendrix over the loudspeakers.

They had to shout to be heard, and even with all the racket in the room, when David caught her eye at various times during the meal, it was as if someone had shut off the sound, stopped the air, stopped her heart. The tingling, electrified sensation lasted only a couple of seconds, but it made her skin feel hot; the sense of anticipation was astonishing.

It was her first experience with wanting someone so desperately, and she had her usual unworldly reaction of wanting to hide with embarrassment. It had been building, below her awareness, for days, since he'd kissed her casually in her car. No, it went back further, to the time he was ill and her fantasies had run riot. But here, now, in the crowded, noisy restaurant, with her sons on either side of her and David across the table, sending subtle wordless messages of growing desire, she wanted him with an intensity that was almost painful. There was a dull, sweet ache between her legs, and she felt ashamed that she wanted the dinner over with so that she could be alone with him.

Thank God the boys didn't know what was going on. Bella was amazed at how easily they accepted David; there was talk of term papers and pulling all-nighters and concerts. With his graduate work, David wasn't that far removed from college life himself, and the three of them had a lot in common.

She could see that college life agreed with Alex and Sam. They were good; no, they were thriving. The mother part of her relaxed inside, knowing that it was so.

When the meal was over, a huge piece of chocolate cake was brought over with a single candle in the middle. All the waiters stood in a circle and sang "Happy Birthday." Bella loved the gesture, hated the fact. Forty. Well, not for another week, but still. Forty. Four-oh. The end.

"Thank you," she said with a huge smile. "That was really sweet."

"Wait," Alex said, and brought out a small package. She unwrapped it and inside was a pair of earrings—long, very delicate silver filigree with an amber stone in the middle. They were a little more "artsy" than her other jewelry, but they were lovely. Her eyes filled. Her sons had really made an effort. All those years of reminding them to call their grandparents and send thank-you notes and birthday cards. This year they'd remembered hers without help from anyone.

"Thank you again," she said, blotting under her eyes with a napkin. "I love them."

"Oh, Mom," Sam said, "you're not going to cry, are you?"

"If I want to, I will."

"Mom gets real soppy," Sam told David.

"So I noticed," he said.

Alex picked up one of the earrings. "They're not real silver, but the lady said they wouldn't turn in your ear."

"That's good to know," Bella said.

Sam requested that she put them on and when she did, he said, "All right!"

"Great, Mom," Alex concurred.

"Beautiful," David said, a private message in his eyes. "Like they were designed for you."

"Thanks," she said softly, and then had to look away from him before she started stammering like an idiot.

They dropped the boys off near Alex's dorm. The campus was an unusual one, consisting of individual colleges set apart from each other by forests of pine and redwoods, all on a bluff overlooking the ocean. Bella had often thought that she wanted, in her next life, to go to school there. Tonight, along with the tingling response to David, she was aware of a wistful nostalgia, a feeling of regret as she gazed up at the moon peeking out from behind a pine tree. The sense of a road not traveled.

As the boys got out of the car, Alex asked, "Will we see you in the morning, David?"

"I don't think so. I'm going to give you guys some time alone with your mother. I'll check out the seismological lab on campus. Maybe we can all get together again for dinner?"

"Great," Alex said. "Bye, Mom. See you about ten, okay? Breakfast at Zachery's."

"Don't you have classes?" she said.

Sam gave her a patronizing look. "We can cut one day, Mom. It's not like high school."

"If you say so." She smiled warmly. "Thank you for a beautiful birthday. I love you both."

She watched as the boys walked through the grove, their hands in their pockets, until they disappeared into the evening mist.

Neither she nor David spoke for a while. The night seemed too quiet to break into with words. After a few moments she felt David's hand on her neck, his thumb and forefinger massaging the tension there. His touch was firm and gentle at the same time; it felt wonderful.

"I like your kids," he said. "You did a great job."

"Did I? I always wonder about Sam, why he's so quick to pick a fight."

"It's his nature, I guess."

"It wasn't always. He was the sweetest, most loving little boy. He used to come up to me three or four times a day and look up at me with those huge eyes in that little face and say, 'Mom, I need a hug,' and then we would snuggle and hold tight to each other." She sighed and shook her head. "And then puberty hit, and it was like a stranger entered his body, and it's been hands off ever since. I know it's normal to separate from your mother, but oh, how I miss that sweet little boy he used to be."

"He still loves you, anyone can see that. They both do."

"And I love them. I wish I'd had more." A few moments passed before she spoke again. "This is a really difficult birthday for me, David."

"Tell me why."

"I'm not sure you'll understand."

"Try me."

Looking out into the night, she spoke slowly, trying to verbalize something she'd never tried to express before. "It's as if I feel very connected to the part of me that can make babies. And that part feels . . . let down, somehow. If I'd lived a hundred, even fifty years ago, I probably would have had six or eight children. There would always be a little one around. I like the thought of that."

She frowned. "I think this birthday is hard because it's a new decade. In the next ten years my body will start to dry up, so that there won't even be a chance of any more babies. It's not that I want another, not really, but the fact that I won't have the choice— that really bothers me."

"I wish I could say something to cheer you up."

Bella turned to him. In the moonlight, the planes of her face were shadowed, like smudged charcoal lines on a drawing. "Doesn't it disturb you, David, that I'm older than you? That I've had a long marriage and have two grown kids? That I'm approaching middle age?"

He took her hands in his. "Stop, Bella. Please, stop."

"Well, doesn't it bother you?"

"No, it doesn't bother me. I never think of people in terms of how old they are. I mean, who cares?"

"I do. I feel old tonight."

Pulling her hands to his chest, he held them there, hoping whatever he said would be the right thing. "There's eight years between us, that's all. Eight years. That's nothing. I wanted to be an astronomer, remember that. When you study the stars, you think in terms of eons, not years. Compared to the stars, you're a child."

That got a halfhearted smile from her, then she lowered her head, rubbing her cheek against their enjoined hands.

"Bella?

"Hmm?"

"Can we stop talking now?"

She looked up at him, a question in her eyes.

"Let me love you," he said softly.

"Here? In the jeep?"

"I was thinking more in terms of a bed."

"Thank God."

"Here we are." David pulled up in front of a small, unimposing motel. "One of the geologists in Parkfield recommended this place. I'll get us a room. Wait here."

The night had an air of unreality about it, as did

Bella's mood. From near depression back on campus, she now felt like giggling. Almost forty, and this was the first time she was about to check into a motel for illicit purposes. Would wonders never cease?

David was back in a couple of minutes. He retrieved their bags, then opened her door. "Come on. I gave both names, in case the kids have to reach you."

"But they don't know where we are."

"They will tomorrow, won't they?"

"You're right. I'd better answer the phone if it rings," she said, following him around the corner of the two-story building.

"Sneaking around? Lying to your children?" he teased.

"You better believe it. They have absolutely no experience of me with anyone except their father, and I'm not about to burst that bubble. Besides, I'm sure they think of me as an old lady, way past mating."

"Sam already asked if we were sleeping together," David tossed casually over his shoulder.

"What?"

"Here we are. Room 213."

He opened the door and tossed the bags on one of the double beds. The room was a typical motel room, with the exception that both beds had brass-railed headboards. Bella remained in the doorway, still digesting David's previous remark, so he ushered

her into the room, closing the door behind them. As
he turned on a light by the bed, he grinned. "I guess
you're not such an old lady after all."

"What did you say when he asked?"

"I said we weren't. At that moment it was true."

"I'm amazed," she said, shaking her head with
wonder. "I thought—"

"Bella. Stop thinking."

He sat on the edge of the bed and pulled her to
him so that she stood between his legs. Taking her
hands, he placed them on his shoulders, then put
his own on her waist. His thumbs reached beneath
the elastic waistband of her culottes to stroke her
hipbone. He looked up at her face. "You okay?"

"Mostly. I'm not sure what to do."

"We could start by taking off our clothes."

"You mean right away?"

"I hope so. I can't wait to see that Italian-film-
star body. I've been-a dreaming about it," he said in
a mock-Italian accent, "it feels-a like forever."

She laughed; he felt her body begin to relax as
she did. "Your accent is awful," she said. "Stick to
rocks. Oh."

His strokes moved from her hipbones over her
velvety stomach, easing the fabric away so he could
massage the area gently. When his fingers found the
first soft curls of her womanhood, her body quivered
under his hands, and he felt a shudder of his own.
He reminded himself that he wanted to take it slow,

even as he wondered if he would be able to do that. The feel of Bella's plush curves already had the blood pounding in his ears.

He rose from the bed and cupped her wide-eyed face in his hands. "How about we take a shower?"

She sighed and leaned against him. "Yes."

With his arm around her, they walked into the bathroom. He seated her on the edge of the tub and, after planting small kisses all over her face, slowly, lovingly, he undressed her. Earrings, sweater, culottes. The removal of each article brought a new round of kisses to the now-exposed skin.

Bella forgot the meaning of the word *embarrassment*. Under David's tender ministrations she felt beautiful. She closed her eyes, heady with the sensation of being celebrated. His kisses were magical—his mouth alternately soft and firm, an occasional loving taste from his tongue. But always with exquisite gentleness. She knew he'd set this leisurely pace so that she could loosen up, and it was working.

By the time David unhooked her lacy bra and tossed it on the floor, then rolled down the matching undies, Bella heard herself panting softly.

Her eyes flew open as he pulled her to a standing position, then stood back and looked at her as if he were a man feasting his eyes on a miracle.

He couldn't believe it. His fantasy woman—every detail exactly as he had imagined it—stood right in front of him. The perfect hourglass. High, full breasts, with large nipples now standing in rosy peaks. The indented waist, the not-quite-flat stomach. Smooth, rounded arms and thighs and hips, with skin like olive-hued satin and a dark, generous, mysterious thatch of curls between her thighs. Hers was a ripe, lush body, made for loving. Sensual, she was so sensual. And tonight she was his.

His breath hissed between his teeth, he wanted her so badly, and he could feel his surging arousal straining against his jeans.

Quickly, he turned on the shower and removed his own clothes. Then he stood looking at her again, unable to take his eyes off her.

"You're so beautiful," she said.

"I think that's my line."

"But it's true. I love your body."

She reached out her arms, and he pulled her to him, the contact enough to make him groan with wanting her. It took all his strength to contain himself, to give them the time to bathe before he plunged into her.

In the shower he let her wash his hair, though he had to bend in half so that she could get to the top of his head. Then he soaped her with long, firm strokes, learning the secrets of her body, while—even with the hot water splaying all around them—she shivered and trembled with every stroke.

David dried Bella off afterward, using the towel to tease and arouse—under her arms, along the soft flesh of her inner wrists. Each toe, then up her calf. Down her back to her flaring buttocks, stroking up and down between the two generous globes.

"David, I can't stand up anymore," Bella said with a gasp, her body quivering as she writhed slowly from his loving attention. Taking her by the hand, he led her into the bedroom and eased her onto the bed. She stretched out there and he bent over and touched his fingertips to her face. By the lamp's soft light, her skin was rosy and her nipples were taut. Her eyes closed as he continued stroking down the length of her, running his palms over the curves of her lush outline as he'd wanted to do from the first.

He settled himself on the edge of the bed, and the movement made her eyes flutter open. Her mouth parted invitingly as she ran her tongue over her lips.

Groaning, he took that full, red mouth, and plunged his tongue into its depths. Her lips were soft and warm. Inside, it was hot and wet and inviting. She moaned and met his thrusts with her own. He was on fire, and he took possession of her, as though she were a prize he had captured. He couldn't get enough of looking at her, touching her, every part of her— face, arms, breasts, between her legs—till he felt her squirming restlessly and heard her calling his name.

"David," Bella cried out through a haze of sensations. Her body wouldn't—couldn't—stop moving. All over, every inch of skin on fire. She opened her eyes to look into his—their strange, pale green trans-lucence pinning her with their intensity. He watched her as he sucked on her nipples till she moaned; she felt his gaze boring into her soul as her head writhed back and forth on the pillow, her nails digging into his shoulders.

"David! Please."

He moved his hand between her thighs and inserted one long finger into the moist heat there. She groaned and opened her legs for him.

"You're so ready for me."

"Oh, yes!"

"I wish I could wait."

"For heaven's sake, why?"

Suddenly he was over her, on her, in her, all the way in her, so that she gasped loudly. It had been so long, she could feel him stretching her, relentless in his need to fill her to the hilt.

"Am I hurting you?"

"No," she said. "Oh, no. David!"

"You're so tight." He grunted, withdrawing, then plunging in again. "Oh, Bella, you feel so good."

He had begun slowly and deliberately, but his rhythm accelerated almost immediately as she matched his movements with her hips. Reaching under her thighs, he pulled her legs up and around his waist. Her heels pressed against the back of his legs. So deep! He was so deep!

But it still wasn't enough. He rose to his knees,

tilting her body upward even more, and plunged into her again. And again. She didn't know how much more she could take. She reached behind her, grabbed the brass rails, and held tight as sensation piled on top of sensation as he drove into her again and again, till she thought she would explode.

"Bella," David whispered in her ear, his breathing raspy and unsteady. "Bella, let go. Please, let go!"

"I . . . oh, yes. Yes!"

And she let it go. All the passion, all the tension of waiting, all the years without love, she released it all with one long cry that went on and on and on. And when it seemed it would finally die out, she felt his pulsating, throbbing release deep inside her, and a cry rose again in her throat to join his.

He eased his body off her, brought the covers up over both of them, and pulled her to him. Bella rested her head against his still rapidly beating heart. "Are you all right?" he asked softly.

"Very much all right."

"Good." He kissed her forehead, and heard her sigh. Her breath was warm against his cooling skin.

Never. It had never been like that. What had happened was a totally new kind of experience for him. It had been . . . intimate; his emotions had been involved, something that he had never allowed to happen in the past. His mind as well as his body had made love to her. He'd felt *connected* in a way that transcended the purely physical. He felt connected now. And whole. And . . . at peace.

He laughed suddenly, a low chuckle.

"What?" Bella said.

"I'm happy."

"Oh, David. So am I."

He squeezed her shoulder. "I have a confession to make," he said.

She lifted her head and looked at him. "Should I be worried?"

"That depends. It's about the motel."

Bella's gaze took in the small, utilitarian room. "Well, it's probably not a four-star place, but it seems to have the basics."

He tucked her head under his chin again. "The thing is, it's pretty old. It was built before the new earthquake consciousness. It's one of the few motels in the world where you can get a room right on top of an active fault."

"What?"

"And for under fifty a night too."

Bella pushed herself away and sat up, clutching the sheet over her breasts. "You're kidding, right?"

He shook his head. "The guy in the office told me the fault line runs through the parking lot, then goes under the building, near the ice machine—"

"The ice machine," she repeated.

"—and comes out again at Room 235."

"And we're in Room 213."

"Yes," he said happily.

"Does that mean it runs under our room?"

"Well, say next door, Room 215. I didn't think you'd want to be right on top of it."

"That was gracious of you. I feel much better."

Her eyes were shooting sparks of indignation at him, her mouth pursed with displeasure. So much fire—he couldn't get over his luck at having this intense, passionate, beautiful woman in his bed. She had no idea, he was sure, that when she was indignant, she was the picture of enticing eroticism.

"Are you angry?" he asked, reaching up and smoothing the tip of one of her nipples through the sheet. "I was kind of hoping you'd be amused, like I am."

Her indrawn breath told of her immediate arousal at his touch, but she said, "You're *amused*, huh? How can you be? We're on top of an earthquake fault!"

With his fingertip he traced lightly around the suddenly aroused bud, watching it grow harder, feeling his own heated reaction starting up again. "The whole state is on an earthquake fault, Bella. Don't worry. This area has a very low probability for eruption."

The sheet fell to her waist. She closed her eyes and moaned softly.

"At least tonight," he amended, his mouth suddenly dry.

She raised her lids in a halfhearted attempt at protest. "Now I really feel relaxed."

"Good." He took both of her breasts in his hands, kneading them gently and watching her breathing rate accelerate. "Now it's time for a one-hundred-eighty-degree turn."

"Huh?"

"It's time to get you unrelaxed," he said softly.

"Again?" She stroked up and down his arms with her nails, and he felt his blood quicken with desire.

"And again, if time and energy permit."

"I didn't know . . ."

"What?" With the palms of his hands he teased her nipples some more, so that they stood out from the lushness of her breasts like deep red pearls.

"That people made love more than once a night," she said on a deep sigh.

"I don't know about people. All I know is, being here with you, this close to you, I don't want to do anything else." He shifted his hand down to the already moist area between her legs and stroked her lightly, tauntingly.

"David!"

"Yes?"

"What if there's an earthquake?"

"We probably won't notice."

This time was far less leisurely than the first. Bella was openly aroused and not in the least embarrassed, while David, knowing the treasure that awaited him, couldn't wait to feel her inner muscles clenching around him again.

They reached for each other with an urgency that made them both laugh, laughter that turned to breathless gasps. In a matter of seconds David was on his back and she was settled on top of him, astride him, as he thrust up into her slick, hot passage.

With his thumbs he stroked the swollen nub of female flesh nestled in her black curls, making her moan and pant loudly as she tightened around him. His strong hands held her steady for the upward thrusts of his straining shaft, repeatedly, tirelessly, relentlessly. And all the while he watched her face—that astonishing face—as she arched back and rode him, twisting and writhing in ecstasy, till the moment when she want suddenly still, then with a strangled cry, went over the edge, her muscles pulsating around him till he knew he was going to die.

He closed his eyes only at the last moment as his body bucked with frenzy and the hot gush of his release exploded within her.

Every fiber of his being throbbed and vibrated for long moments afterward. And through the misty whirlwind of sensations, he remembered that his last thought before his release had been deep regret. For the first time in his life he was bitterly unhappy that his seed was without viability, that he couldn't give a woman a child. This woman. His child. His and Bella's child.

It would never be. It could never be.

He was amazed at the pain that knowledge brought.

EIGHT

Talk about one-hundred-eighty-degree turns, Bella thought. To spend an exhausting, exhilarating, even educational night in her lover's arms, then to stroll around the campus of U.C. Santa Cruz the next day with her sons, trying hard to keep all evidence of how she'd spent the night before from her face or conversation.

She'd thought she'd be a wreck. She and David had had no more than two hours sleep. All that loving, she thought, a delicious chill spreading over her at the thought. So much loving—how many times she had no idea, as she'd lost count somewhere before dawn—surely it had to show, to be emblazoned on her like a tattoo. But the boys didn't seem to notice any change in her demeanor as Alex walked her and Sam around the campus, pointing out various buildings and landmarks that had meaning to him.

A strange-looking metal sculpture on a small

knoll near Porter College was nicknamed the Flying I.U.D. The school mascot was a banana slug, of all things, which was why the coffee shop they passed was named the Hungry Slug. They toured the beautiful new science library and a couple of colleges under construction, and all the while Bella smiled and nodded, even laughed in the appropriate places so they wouldn't know. But it was hard to stay in the present when the recent past had been so memorable.

She understood now that what she had thought of as giving in to sexual needs was not that at all. She had given into love. She loved David—her nature was such that she could not have shared the night with him, letting him transport her to a whole new plane as he had, without there being love. Not for her the impersonal coupling, the physical-only sexual gymnastics, the scratching of an itch without thoughts of the consequences. She wasn't made that way. She could have come away with David and spent the night with him, letting down her guard and her inhibitions, only because she loved him.

She wouldn't tell him, of course. At least not yet. It would probably scare him half to death. What did he feel? she wondered as she browsed around the bookstore with the boys. David had said he was incapable of the emotion of love, but surely, what they had together had *some* meaning. Didn't it? Couldn't he, wouldn't he, love her? Was he able?

It was a sobering question. One that, as she and the boys had lunch at The Howling Cow Cafe on campus, she couldn't seem to stop asking herself. And it put a damper on her previously high mood.

It was time for a reality check, she told herself sternly. There had never been any doubt about how it would turn out. David might enjoy her company, David might lust after her, David might even make love to her as if she were the sexiest, most desirable woman in the universe, but David didn't feel comfortable with relationships. He'd told her that from the beginning and as recently as the drive up the day before.

Still . . .

There was that small, hopeful inner voice again, and it couldn't help asking if, before it was over, mightn't he learn to love her just a little?

Did he love her? David wondered at various times during the day—exploring the lab on campus, climbing over some cracked concrete and debris still left in town from the quake four years before. Is love what that feeling was? If it was, it was frightening. Intense, too intense. It invaded him, obliterating the ability to think straight, and David didn't like anything that interfered with his thought processes. Oh, it was all right during sex—hell, it was good to turn your mind off then. But not at any other time.

All these feelings, all these mood swings every time he remembered the night before with Bella. He was like some kind of pubescent kid—up and down, hot and cold, joyful, sad. Extremes. Too much. Way too much.

He stood on the pier and looked out at the Pacific Ocean. It was a gorgeous, sunny day with a slight autumn chill in the air. With his hands in his back pockets, he looked out at the small boats in the bay and tried to analyze his feelings for Bella. That was his training, after all, to break down the components of a given situation and study them in relation to the whole.

He was drawn to her face, her body. She made him laugh. Her mind was a good one—even with her lack of higher education, she was both logical and street smart. He missed her when she wasn't there. He missed her right now, resented the time she was spending alone with her sons, even though he knew it was the right thing to do for all concerned.

She turned him on all the time—sleeping, waking, eating. Even brushing her teeth. Just that morning, while she was bent over the sink in the motel bathroom, he'd been unable to resist coming up behind her and cupping her breasts in his hands, then stroking downward till he reached the moist velvet folds between her legs. Her reaction had been immediate, as had been his, and he took her right there, standing up, her mouth full of toothpaste as she held on to the sides of the sink while he poured himself into her.

Never. It had never been like this with anyone before, this craving for a woman, this . . . voraciousness, this depth of passion and sensation. Was this what it was like to be in love?

And was it normal to be terrified at the thought?

That night, after they said their good-byes to the boys—both Sam and Alex had shook his hand, then hugged him good-bye, making David choke up for a moment—he and Bella were silent with each other, wrapped up in their own thoughts and unable or unwilling to share them.

Their silence lasted until they got back to the motel. The minute they got into the room, she reached for him and he groaned. How could he want her so much? Again?

But he did. That night they were even more unrestrained with each other, and again it went on into the morning. According to Bella, her and Jake's sex life had been satisfying, but rather conventional, and she laughingly told David that she expected him—as a younger man—to introduce her to all the variations of lovemaking. He was most glad to oblige; she was most glad to learn. They didn't start back to Los Angeles until late Wednesday afternoon because it was necessary that they get a little sleep before embarking on the six-hour drive.

On the way home they talked lightly of the boys, the campus, the weather. As though there were an unspoken agreement between them, they steered away from anything more intimate.

When they pulled into the driveway, David suggested that he spend that night alone in the guest house, and she agreed, but then he made the mistake of kissing her good night and somehow he wound up in her bedroom. That wonderful king-size bed had all the space the motel room bed had lacked, and they took full advantage of it.

When the morning came, and it was time for him to go to Santa Monica, he reluctantly dragged himself away from the warmth of her embrace. Bella offered to cook him breakfast and he accepted, eating twice as much as he usually did and letting her fuss over him a little bit.

What scared him was that he didn't mind.

Looking in the mirror, Bella adjusted the broad-brimmed hat so that it sat comfortably on her head. A hat! How much fun to wear a hat again. When she decided the angle had just the right amount of jauntiness, she stepped back to take in the whole outfit, and was arrested suddenly by what she saw in the glass.

It was her mother looking back at her. Bella had few childhood memories, as she'd been so young when she'd been separated from her parents, but still she remembered Mama as an inveterate hat-wearer. Bella would sit on her parents' bed and gaze adoringly as her mother would slant the brim one way, then another, finally sticking huge pearl-topped pins through the hat's crown, into her chignon.

My mother's face, she thought wistfully. *It's true; we do turn into our mothers.*

After adjusting her hose and smoothing down the skirt, she turned around to make sure her slip wasn't showing. It was a wonderful outfit—a loose hunter-green jacket draped over a teal blue and green silk print—and she was glad she'd bought it. Kate's wedding deserved a special dress, and Bella knew she looked good. She wasn't even upset about her birthday the next day. What were numbers, after all? David certainly didn't treat her like an old lady. Far from it.

She was aware that her face glowed as she put on a shiny coral lipstick—the glow of a well-satisfied woman. Kate had shone with that same radiance since she and T.R. had decided to get married.

Bella was really looking forward to Kate's wedding. She'd seen her friend through all the years when she struggled to raise Dee alone, then through the rocky courtship with T.R. Speaking of rocky courtships, Bella had also been around to give love and comfort to Hollis when she and Tony had some stormy times. The three women friends had spent many a coffee break comparing notes on men, and how seemingly impossible it was to find a good one.

Of course, for most of that time, Bella hadn't had a lot to contribute. Until—

"Bella?"

Speak of the devil, she thought with a smile, making one final adjustment to her hair. David had let himself in the back door with his key.

"Coming," she called out.

Slipping into her three-inch heels, she swept through the hallway into the kitchen, checking the contents of her small silk purse.

She looked up as she entered the room, then stopped short. "David. You're not dressed."

He wore the ubiquitous jeans and T-shirt and was leaning against the wall by the back door, his arms folded over his chest. She'd expected him to be in a suit and tie, or barring that, a sports jacket, at least.

"I'm not trying to criticize you," she said, smiling, "really I'm not. But it *is* a wedding. I don't think—"

He interrupted her. "I'm not going, Bella."

"Excuse me?"

"I'm not going to be able to go to the wedding. A last-minute emergency came up at the site, and the whole crew is meeting there in an hour."

For a moment she couldn't think of a thing to say. "I see," she managed finally.

He uncrossed his arms and raked all ten fingers through his hair. "I don't mean to hang you up, but it isn't like my not being there will affect anything. You were kind of dragging me along anyway, weren't you? I hardly know Kate, and I've never met what's-his-name."

"T.R.," she said absently, noting David's defensiveness and wondering if she'd done anything to cause it. "No, it won't affect anything. I'll miss you, that's all."

"Yeah, well . . ." He looked down and shifted his feet, as though he wanted to get away but didn't know how to do it gracefully.

"David," she said. "Is there anything else? Something you're not telling me?"

He looked up. There was a flash of concern on his face. No, not concern. Guilt.

He shrugged and shook his head. "No. It's just . . . I'm sorry."

She wondered what he was sorry for, but he wasn't about to tell her, she could see that.

"It's all right, David. Really it is." Looking down, she fumbled with her purse clasp. "Will I see you later?"

"I'm not sure when I'll be in."

"All right." Lifting her head, Bella stood tall. There was no way she was going to cling or whine or pout. No way. "Well, have a good time." She gave him what she hoped was a confident smile. "I sure intend to."

The wedding was held at a ranch in Malibu owned by one of T.R.'s musician friends. Under a huge hanging willow tree by a winding country road, the bride and groom exchanged vows. The wind was as strong as the sun, and Bella had to hold on to her hat as she, along with several others, watched Kate and T.R. promise to nurture and care for each other. A sigh went through the group of assembled guests— Kate's family, a couple of T.R.'s friends, Bella, and Hollis from the shop.

Dee cried throughout the whole thing. They were happy tears, and the teenager was enfolded in the embrace of Kate's mother, Claire, whose eyes were a bit misty too.

Hollis—with Tony's strong arms around her— smiled nostalgically, as though remembering her own special day.

Kate had T.R. Hollis had Tony. Dee had Claire. And Bella had . . . no one. It was supposed to have been David next to her, his arm around her, his mouth kissing her tears away.

Cut the self-pity, she admonished herself. *Cut it out right now*.

What a fool she was not to have seen it sooner.

The last couple of days he'd been giving her signs. His moods were erratic. First he would say he needed time alone, then he would change his mind. He took her out to dinner every night, telling her she didn't need to keep cooking for him. There were more silences now. He was pulling away, trying to put some distance between them. It wasn't unexpected, of course, but she hadn't thought it would happen so soon.

He wasn't tired of her in bed, she knew that. But still, his lovemaking the last couple of times had been tinged with desperation, as though he were waging an internal war of some sort. He was relentless in making sure she was satisfied, more than once, every time they made love. It was as though he were showing that at least in this area he was able to give to her.

But he never talked about what was going on, and when she tried to introduce the subject, he shut down even more.

No, this was not unexpected.

But that didn't mean it didn't hurt.

The service was over, and the bride and groom kissed. Kate's face, as she looked at her new husband, was lit up with love. Bella's gaze went to Hollis— she, too, glowed with love for Tony. A surge of jealousy twisted in Bella's breast, as unexpected as it was sudden. What was the matter with her? She never resented other people's happiness. There was too little of that in the world to wish it away, for anyone.

Oh, David.

Tears rolled down her cheeks, and she wiped them with her hanky. Hollis put her hand on her arm, and Bella smiled shakily, knowing that her friend assumed she was crying over the beauty of love.

But she knew she was crying instead for its loss.

She peered in the window of the guest house bedroom. He was lying on his bed, his hands folded behind his head, staring at the ceiling. She wondered how long he'd been home. She wondered if he'd left at all.

She tapped on his window, startling him. Giving her a weak smile, he sat up and scratched his head. She walked over to the front door which, a few seconds later, he opened for her. "Hi," he said. "Just get home?"

"Just."

He stood back as she came through the door. She liked this room, with its plump sofa and antique sideboard and brick-lined fireplace. She'd furnished it herself, and it was a friendly, comforting place. Not today though. There would be no comfort for her here today.

"How was the wedding?" David asked.

"It was beautiful. The day was perfect, not too hot but sunny. You would have— I mean, it was really nice. How was your day?"

She was uncomfortable about something, David observed, and was doing her usual mental scurrying around before she hit on the words. He wished he could ease whatever it was that was bothering her, but he'd been so screwed up himself lately, he didn't think he had anything to offer.

He walked over to the fireplace and bent down to light the fire. It was almost October and the late afternoons were starting to get a little chilly. "Would you like a drink?" he asked. "I think I have some scotch and a couple of beers."

"I'd like a scotch. Two cubes, please."

"Sit down, okay? Your standing up like that is making me nervous."

He fixed them both a drink, then seated himself next to her on the sofa. He wanted to take her into his arms and hold her, but his invisible shield was up, the one he'd created in childhood, the one where he felt wrapped in cellophane—he could observe the world, but no one could touch him. He knew from her eyes that she felt it, his distance, and it bothered her.

She sipped her drink, then set it down on the coffee table. "David?"

"That's my name," he said, then winced at how flip he sounded.

"I was hurt today that you didn't want to go to the wedding."

"Bella, I—"

"No, let me finish."

Nodding, he said, "Okay."

"At first I thought it was rude of you, that you should have given me notice. Then I wondered if you even had to go to the site, or if you were using it as an excuse. Then"—she took another sip of her drink, as though she needed fortification—"I thought some more about it, and I understood. Or at least, I think I did. The wedding made you nervous, didn't it? Seeing two people commit to a lifetime together was too uncomfortable for you. Am I close?"

Close? She'd hit the bull's-eye. "You're in the neighborhood."

"And then I thought, why is that such a big deal? It's not as if we've ever talked about marriage, or anything else to do with committing to each other. I haven't asked it of you, or expected it of you, so why should you feel threatened?"

"Bella—"

She held her hand up. "Let me get all this out, and then we can talk about it. I decided that you were uncomfortable because maybe you thought I *did* expect that from you, and you were feeling confined. You obviously don't have those kind of feelings for me. You've been giving me some pretty broad hints, and I'm not stupid."

Her eyes filled and she wiped at them angri-ly. "Dammit, I promised myself I was not going to cry."

He reached a hand out to her, but she shook her head and went on, her face set in determina-tion. "Look, I know we're too different, emotionally, temperamentally, age-wise. I have grown children, for God's sake. I truly have never thought of us as . . . long-term. But you don't even seem to want something short-term.

"I don't take it personally, you know, David—that you don't want to get involved with *me*. I think you don't want to get involved with *anyone*. So I think your not going to the wedding with me today was your way of telling me that you're getting ready to end it—you and me . . . us, whatever that is—and so I thought I'd come here and end it first. And that's what I have to say."

She expelled a huge breath and looked down at her hands. Then she lifted her glass and drained its contents. Still she didn't meet his eyes and sat, cradling the empty glass in her hand.

He felt awful. It was obvious that he had caused her pain. Hell, he'd caused himself pain. And he didn't know what to do about it.

"Bella," he began, choosing his words carefully. "I don't want to end it."

She looked up, hope flaring in her eyes. "You don't?"

"No, I don't. You're too important to me. I mean, you're right that I felt threatened by the wedding, by being with you there and having your friends think . . . you know, that we're together."

"I don't understand. What do you call what we've been doing this past week, if not being together?"

"I'm not really sure. I know I feel things for you that I've never felt before. But I don't know what to do with that. I don't know where to put that."

"Why does it have to be put anywhere?"

"Because it does." He got up from the couch, too restless to stay seated. "I need to understand things, or else I get unsettled. Emotions are messy. I never know what to do with them."

"You *feel* emotions, David. That's what you do with them."

"Yeah. Well, I've been feeling, and I'm about to jump out of my skin."

He felt his heart pounding against his chest and suddenly he wanted to be out of that room, somewhere in the wilderness, alone. Safe.

Several moments went by as he leaned on the fireplace mantel and stared into the flames.

From behind him he heard Bella ask, "What do you want from me, David?"

He turned. "Huh?"

"You heard me." Her gaze was steady.

"Damned if I know. What do you want from me?"

"The truth?" she asked.

"Yes."

"I want you to try to make a go of it. To try to . . . love me. I already love you, I'm afraid. I have from the beginning, I think."

"How do you know? How do you know you love me?"

"How do I breathe?" she shot back. "I just know."

He nodded. "Yeah. You have the gift, don't you."

He paced up and down in front of the fireplace, thinking, trying to make some sense out of the emotions swirling through him in turbulent waves. Finally, he stopped pacing and leaned against the mantel and stared at her. "I can't, Bella. I'm sorry," he said, shaking his head slowly.

She raised huge, bruised eyes to him. "You don't love me, even a little?" she asked softly, then shook her head angrily, as though castigating herself. "No! Forget I said that."

Setting her glass down on the coffee table, she rose hurriedly. "I have to go now."

She was at the door by the time he caught up to her and turned her around. "No, I don't want to lose you. I can't lose you. Can't we just forget the whole love thing? Can't we just go on like we have been?"

"I'm afraid it's too late. The words have been spoken." Her eyes were as dull as her voice. "I've told you I love you, and you've told me you don't.

It would be too upsetting for me to keep seeing you, sleeping with you, knowing what I know now."

He held on to her for a moment longer, then dropped his arms to his sides. "Yeah, I guess it would."

Her eyes searched his face, as if trying to find some clue to him there. Then she turned and put her hand on the doorknob. Her movement was arrested, and her head dropped dispiritedly. "It would be nice if I were one of those terribly modern women who wouldn't mind if an ex-lover still lived on the property, but I'm not like that. Not modern at all. I think it would be better if you moved out."

"All right."

She turned to him, concern on her face. "You did say your friend John could put you up, didn't you? I mean, it's not as if you have nowhere to stay."

He wondered if it was possible to be any more moved by another human being than he was by Bella. "Don't," he said softly, miserable. "Don't kick me out and then worry about where I'm going. Don't do that to yourself. I can take care of myself."

She smiled bleakly. "Yes, you can, can't you? You've told me that all along. That's it, then."

"I'll be out by tomorrow."

"If you say so."

Again she turned to leave, and again she turned back to him. "I guess this is real progress."

"How?"

"This whole conversation has been extremely uncomfortable for me . . . and not once did I offer you anything to eat."

Smiling tremulously, she walked out the door.

NINE

Bella wiped her eyes impatiently, never halting the rhythm of her rocking chair. The baby in her arms was so thin—a crack baby, undernourished, possibly brain damaged. It would probably be merciful, Bella told herself, if the little one died. Her mother was unable to care for her and she was most likely unadoptable.

And still Bella couldn't seem to stop crying. She looked around her surreptitiously; it wouldn't do to have the nurses here on the preemie ward see her weeping over one of the babies. She was supposed to provide calm, nurturing warmth, a little love. Not tears. Tears that flowed as much for herself as for the doomed child in her arms.

When would it stop hurting? she wondered. When would the disappointment go away? She had thought, foolishly, that since she'd gone into

the affair with David with her eyes open, the end
wouldn't be too devastating. How wrong could one
human being be?

It had been almost a month since she'd seen
him.

True to his word, he'd been out of the guest
house the next day. She didn't even know where
he'd gone. He'd left no word at all. How could
he do that, not even let her know where he was?
A few days after their parting, she had wanted to
talk to him, to tell him that she hadn't meant it to
be as final as it sounded. He was still family, after
all. In a while, when she was over him, when she
had stopped loving him, he could still visit, or call,
or come over to dinner. The boys had liked him,
why should they—why should he—be deprived of
family?

No, no, she reminded herself, David didn't get
warm and toasty at the concept of family. His and
her experiences with relatives, with holidays, with
religion, had been diametric opposites. She always
went toward connectedness; he ran from it as if it
were the plague.

And so he'd been gone a month.

Her birthday had come and gone, strangely anti-
climactic. Probably because she'd mourned enough
before the fact, the reality wasn't as bad as the expectation. The women in the shop had thrown her
a surprise luncheon, showering her with gag gifts.

Hollis had taken her to the ballet. Kate, back from her honeymoon in Hawaii, had brought with her an exquisite coral necklace and earrings.

She'd spoken to Alex and Sam a couple of times in the past month. Each had asked about David and, in as neutral a voice as possible, she'd told them that he had moved on, and promised she'd say hello to him from them the next time they spoke.

David's absence seemed especially disappointing to Sam, who had always been her difficult child. Bella sensed some unhappiness in him, a restless irritability that usually meant he was struggling with something. She tried to get him to talk to her about it, but, as usual, he shut her out. She wondered if—hoped— there was some older student or teacher at Berkeley that he could talk to. Now that Jake was gone, there was no mature male figure in his life; had David stuck around, he might have been someone her son could talk to. But David hadn't stuck around.

Both boys promised to come home for Thanksgiving, and Bella looked forward to it like a lifeline. Family holidays were the best cure for heartaches.

The child in her arms twitched a little and her breathing sounded troubled. Bella looked down into the baby's pinched face. Was it an emergency or just a bad dream? The child was too pale, even paler than when Bella had first arrived that day.

She rose from the rocking chair and found a nurse, who took one look at the baby and swooped her away to the surgical area behind double swinging doors. Bella wished she could go there too, to be part of whatever happened to that lost little child. But it wasn't her domain. She had done all she could, she knew that, and left with a strong sense that the next time she came to hug preemies, that baby girl wouldn't be there.

As always, she tried to accept death with resignation, but today it hurt even more. She was still pretty raw from David's leaving, still pretty vulnerable to all the pain in the world. She'd been unable even to look at the evening news—famine, starvation, wars.

Pain. Too much pain.

She stood waiting for the elevator, and she wondered if David felt it too. She could almost feel his presence right at that moment, which didn't really surprise her. She'd been connected to him, plugged into him, since she'd first laid eyes on him. Oh, yes, David was in pain, the same way she was. But was he allowing himself to feel it? Or had he closed up again—was he armored, shielded once more from his own human nature?

David, she sighed silently as she stepped onto the elevator. David, where are you?

She walked toward him, her skirts swishing around her legs, generous hips swaying in a dance of sensuality, those full breasts bobbing slightly, straining against the

*buttons of her blouse, taunting him with their lushness,
begging him to cup them in his hands, begging him to
drown in her. Smiling mysteriously, she reached out a
beckoning hand, and he tried to grasp it, but she began
to fade, to become part of the mist. He ran after her, but
she kept fading and fading.*

"Bella!" David cried out. "No! Don't go away!"

He sat up, gasping erratically and completely
disoriented. He looked at his surroundings with no
recognition; it was as though he'd been dropped onto
a strange planet.

He was in a tent, in a sleeping bag. All around
him lay his gear—tools, backpack, notebooks. It was
night. Strange chirpings, hissings, a rhythmic clicking
sound was all he could hear on the other side of
the canvas. As his breathing returned to normal, he
remembered.

He was in a forest high in the Chilean mountains,
near the spot he'd left weeks before. He'd returned
there after work on the trench in Santa Monica had
been completed and the carbon samples had been
sent off to the lab. He could have hung around in
L.A., waiting for results, but he needed to get away,
away from Bella, away from memories.

His mind drifted back to that time, weeks earlier. After he moved out of the guest house, he kept
telling himself he was all right. And he was, during
the day at least. He worked harder than he ever had
before. The light determined his hours, and he was

there at the site from sunup to sundown. When darkness fell, he took long walks on the beach, or read a scientific journal. Once in a while he had a drink with the others, but not often.

For the first time in his life he found himself watching TV. John's wife had offered the pull-out couch in their den, and the TV remote control had come in handy when the sleepless nights became a regular happening.

As though he were taunting himself, he drove by Bella's shop a couple of times a week, always on the days he knew she was there, but he never stopped in. Finally, he'd hopped a plane back to Chile and rejoined the geologic team he'd been with before he'd first come to L.A. The move had been a geographic solution to what he suspected was a nongeographic problem—something along the lines of: out of sight, out of mind.

But she was never out of his mind. Especially at night. Damn, he thought, wearily wiping his hand over his face, it was bad and getting worse. If he wasn't careful, he could get sick.

He undid his canteen and took a swig of water. The nights, the terrible nights. She invaded his sleep, his dreams, his very soul. The dreams varied, from him running, panicked, through strange streets, trying to find something that he couldn't name, to the overtly sexual, like the one he'd had that evening. He would wake up from one of those, rock-hard with wanting her, and restless because no matter what he might do to relieve himself, nothing took the place of Bella. Nothing and no one.

Chris, the graduate student on the Santa Monica dig, had come on pretty strong to him several times. She'd even offered her services, as a geologist and a bed partner, in Chile. Ordinarily, he would have taken her up on her not-too-subtle invitation. They could share their common interest during the day and give each other some comfort at night. Chris was the kind he could be with for a while and then move on without ever looking backward, which was what women had always been for him.

Not that he'd left a slew of broken hearts behind. With unerring instinct, he had honed in on the ones who weren't looking for any more heavy involvement than he was. When it was over, it was mutual, and no one lost any sleep over it.

From the beginning it had been different with Bella. She was the one he couldn't forget. Not even when he slept.

Sleep. Damn. When would he get a good night's sleep again? He raked his fingers through his hair, feeling how long and shaggy he'd let it get. The beard was back too. Bella had liked his beard, but she should see him now. He knew he looked like hell, and he had a hard time giving a damn.

Bella. When he closed his eyes, he could see her, soft and warm and generous, the invitation in her eyes urging him to come closer. Then her expression changed, her eyes now wounded, as they'd looked the evening they had parted.

She was too damned vulnerable, too trusting. She was as readable as a book, accessible, and he secretly envied that open quality in her. There was no detour between what she felt and what she showed—it was always immediate. When Bella was happy, you knew it right away; when she was sad, the same. And when she was turned on, it was obvious, and strong, and more sensual than any other woman could possibly be.

Sometimes he found himself angry at her for sending him away, for not giving him more time to adjust to all the new feelings. But then he remembered that he was the one who had said he didn't want to give it a try, to try to love her. She had released him, and he had run like hell.

Was he an emotional cripple? he asked himself. Was his life going to be one of restless wandering, never putting down roots, never having a special, close, important *other* to share with? All his life he had thought and said that was the way he wanted it.

But not since Bella.

Bella.

Groaning, he lay back down and tried to sleep. An owl hooted; somewhere in the distance, an animal screeched loudly. All the night sounds seemed exaggerated, all the thoughts in his head screamed at him. After a while he cursed and threw the cover back. Fumbling around in his backpack, he found a small flask and helped himself to a swig of brandy. Lately, it was the only way he could knock himself out. A pretty stupid way, he knew that. Drinking yourself into oblivion was about as foolish as . . . letting a woman like Bella get away.

"Whose idea was it to have Russian food this month?" Bella asked.

Hollis, who was happily chewing on a piece of black bread, moved her head to indicate Kate.

"Yup, it was me," Kate said. "Isn't it delicious?"

The three friends had dinner one Sunday a month at a different ethnic restaurant. Tonight they were in the Fairfax area of Los Angeles, where a lot of recent Russian immigrants had settled, in an eating establishment that had been recommended as a best bet in the *Times.*

"I'm afraid it's not sitting too well in my stomach," Bella said.

"What's the matter?" Hollis asked, wiping around her mouth daintily with her napkin. "Don't you like your caraway dumplings? I think they're delicious."

"It must be me," Bella said, swallowing down her queasiness. "Nothing's been tasting right lately."

Kate and Hollis exchanged worried looks. "You haven't been looking at all well, you know," Hollis said. "You're pale, and there are circles under your eyes. It's David, isn't it?"

Kate added, "I don't care what you say, you're still not over him."

"I'm fine."

"Hey, this is me, Kate, and Hollis. Your buddies, remember? You can tell us how much you're hurting. You don't have to hold it in."

"I'm not holding it in."

Kate sighed loudly. "Really, Bella, you're impossible. You spend your life taking care of people, but when *you* need taking care of, you never let any of us do anything for you."

Bella closed her eyes as another wave of nausea came over her. "If you'd like to take my digestive system, you're welcome to it."

"Do you need to go to the rest room?" Hollis asked anxiously.

"No, it's passed." Bella opened her eyes and gave her friends a reassuring smile. "And you're right, of course, I do have a hard time letting you comfort me. I'm sorry."

She took a sip of hot tea, hoping it would bring some relief. Putting her cup down, she frowned. "It's just that I worry about him. It's been almost two months, and I don't even know where he is. I called the Geology Department at U.C.L.A. and they said he was out of the country. I hope he's all right."

"And that's all this is?" Kate said skeptically. "Worry about David? Not a broken heart?"

"No," Bella said as firmly as she could, hoping it was so. "It wasn't going to work out anyway—I knew that from the start. It's probably better that it ended so soon."

"And if you believe that, I have a bridge to sell you. Bella . . ." Kate put a reassuring hand on her friend's arm. "Stop being so understanding, so nice. Hate the guy a little. I do. He rejected you."

"But I was the one who ended it."

"Because he said he didn't love you."

"I rushed it. It was too soon. I didn't give him enough time."

"It doesn't take a lot of time," Kate said. "I knew with T.R. pretty soon, even though I fought it. But I knew. And Hollis, when did you know with Tony?"

"The minute he walked into the room," Hollis answered with a gentle smile. "But I admitted it to myself the next day."

Kate turned back to Bella. "You see? Stop making excuses for the guy. He hurt you."

"Not any more than he hurt himself."

"Bella, Bella, Bella. What are we going to do with you?"

"Look," Bella said, "I loved someone who didn't

love me back. Am I supposed to blame him for that? How can I? I have no right."

Kate's expression was speculative before it faded into one of smiling resignation. "I'm sorry. I'm pushing you too much. It's because I hate to see you like this. But look," she added in a firmer tone, "you have every right to be angry, and I don't care if it is irrational. Maybe the fact that you haven't gotten good and pissed off is why your stomach is hurting."

"Nonsense." Bella, more agitated at Kate's words than she was comfortable with, played nervously with a crust of bread. "I think it's something entirely different."

"The flu?" suggested Hollis.

"No. Early menopause."

Kate said, "But you're too young."

"Maybe. But I've missed a period and I'm late for the second. That's one of the signs."

"Might I remind you that it's also a sign of pregnancy?" Hollis suggested tentatively.

"Not possible. I've told you, there's no way."

"And we believe you," Hollis soothed. "Kate, I think we ought to let Bella alone. If she doesn't want to talk to us about David, she shouldn't have to."

"No, it's not that," Bella said. "It's that I don't have any more tears left. I'm drained." Shrugging, she smiled sheepishly. "That's probably why my cycle has been interrupted—too many emotions. Just being here with the two of you is making me feel a lot better. I promise."

"All right," Kate said, nodding. "I'll get off your case. But remember, if you need someone's shoulder to cry on, you'd better call me."

"And then me," Hollis said.

Bella looked at each of them and smiled. "What would I do without the two of you? All right. Enough. Now," she said brightly, picking up the menu, "I suddenly feel a lot better. Let's order something disgusting for dessert."

"I can always be talked into something disgusting," Kate said, smiling also, but the glance she and Hollis shared was far from happy.

On the way home from the restaurant, Bella stopped off at an all-night drugstore to get something to settle her stomach. On her way to the checkout counter, she passed the aisle with the home pregnancy kits. She stopped and smiled. It was silly to even entertain the thought, she told herself. David had had a vasectomy. Still—she'd never used one of these. The boys had been conceived when the medical profession was still talking about waiting for rabbits to die.

On a sudden whim, and feeling decidedly foolish, she added one of the kits to her purchases.

"Now, that's what I call a turkey," Hollis's husband, Tony, said as Bella brought the enormous platter to the table.

It was the night after Thanksgiving, and Bella was throwing her traditional dinner for her friends. She never held it on Thanksgiving Day because everyone else had family to go to. The previous night, Alex, Sam, and Bella had had Chinese takeout while they watched their two favorite movies on the VCR—*Airplane* and *Singin' in the Rain*. By now they were able to recite most of the lines along with the actors on the screen, and the evening had been as special as any family gathering could have been.

Bella smiled at the faces around her huge dining room, which she hardly ever used now. The table-cloth was pale orange, and there was a centerpiece of Indian corn and multicolored squashes. Under the huge chandelier—which Jake had insisted they buy, even though Bella had wanted something less formal—there were twelve at the table: Kate and T.R. and Dee and Claire. Tony and Hollis. Alex and Sam. A couple of manicurists, and a couple of customers from the shop. Bella made thirteen. Unlucky thirteen? Or lucky? Tonight she was sure it was the latter.

"Tony," Bella said, "Hollis says you enjoy playing godfather, so the boys and I have decided you should carve the bird."

Tony's handsome features creased in a smile. "My pleasure."

"I'll bring the rest of the food out while you do that."

"Need any help, Mom?" Alex asked.

Sam, breaking off a hot and heavy argument with Dee on the relative merits of a new rap group, looked up also. "Do you, Mom?"

"Not now. I think I'll put you two to work cleaning up later."

"Me too," said Dee, whose spiked red hair was particularly spiky tonight. "Your kitchen is so cool, it'll be fun."

"You're on," Bella said, beaming at the teenager. She'd known Dee since she was a child and thought of her almost as the daughter she never had.

A daughter, she mused as she returned to the kitchen for the special dishes that meant Thanksgiving. A daughter would be nice. She shook her head and almost laughed out loud.

Pregnant! The doctor had confirmed it. Forty years old, unmarried and respectable, and she was going to have a baby. Instead of despair, the news had made her leap with happiness inside.

A baby! It was a gift, unexpected but not unwanted. She needed a place for all her frustrated maternalism, had needed it for years. She would be very careful, she assured herself, not to get too carried away with her new child. Too much mothering could be as destructive as not enough.

But still, a baby . . .

No one knew yet. She felt that she needed to let David know first. There'd been a postcard from him the week before, from Chile, but he hadn't mentioned where he was going from there, or if he intended to get in touch with her. She sighed, not even surprised at the wave of sadness that washed over her. The news of the expected baby had certainly snapped her out of the depression she'd been in—the depth of which she hadn't even shared with her two best friends—but there was still a lot of feeling there, a sense of loss.

She wondered how he'd take the news, and then, remembering what he'd said about bringing children into the world, smiled sadly because she knew. He wouldn't be thrilled the way she was. Not in the least.

It was all right though. She'd have this child alone and be perfectly happy raising it alone too.

Humming a little tune, she heaped yams and stuffing onto platters. Donning oven mitts, she reached into the oven and removed the corn bread. The aroma was sensational. As she turned to put the pan on a hot rack, she heard a tapping at her kitchen window. At first she thought it was a branch of a tree that the wind sometimes shoved against the side of the house.

Then she heard it again and looked up.

David.

David's face was staring at her from the other side of the window.

The pan of corn bread dropped out of her hands and onto the floor, just missing her feet and scattering all over the linoleum. Dazed, her heart pounding, she looked down to see what had happened, and suddenly David was there, pulling her out of the way and taking her in his arms.

"I'm sorry," he said, his voice husky with emotion. "I didn't mean to scare you. Are you all right?"

"You're here. David, you're here." And Bella burst into tears.

"Mom! What was that noise?" Alex said as he ran into the kitchen followed by Sam, then Kate, then Hollis.

"Bella," Hollis said, "are you—?"

There was a shocked silence as all of them took in the tableau of Bella, sobbing, encircled by David's arms as he murmured, "Hush. It's all right. It's all right."

Kate gathered all the onlookers together and hustled them out of the room, announcing in a loud voice, "Dinner will be delayed a few moments. Anyone want more wine?"

"Where were you?" Bella said into David's plaid shirt. She'd never been happier to see anyone in all her life.

"In a forest on a mountain."

She drew her head back and looked up at him, her eyes shining with tears. "God, you look awful."

"I know. You look beautiful."

"Have you been sick?"

"No. I just haven't taken very good care of myself, that's all."

Her mood switched completely and she found herself beating on his chest with her fists. Was it Kate who had said she needed to get angry? Kate should look at her now. "How could you do it?" Bella said fiercely. "How could you go so far away and not let me know where you were or how you were?"

"I don't know. I'm an idiot."

"I hated you. I hated you so."

He captured her clenched hands in his much larger ones and, although she struggled, he had no trouble pulling and holding them against his shirtfront. "Don't, Bella. Please. I can't stand seeing you upset."

She struggled for a moment longer, then sighed loudly while her sniffling subsided and her anger left her as suddenly as it had sprung up. "Your timing stinks," she said with a final shudder.

"The story of my life," he observed ruefully.

"No, I mean I have all these people here, and I have to serve dinner."

"Good."

He kissed the top of her head, then released her,

grinning. "I'm starving. Let me wash up, and I'll help you. I look like this," he said, glancing down at his threadbare jeans and hiking boots, "because I came here straight from the airport. I didn't know you'd have company."

He walked over to the sink and poured dishwashing detergent on his hands, then thoroughly scrubbed his face, arms, and hands. Drying himself off with a kitchen towel, he looked over his shoulder and said, "Now, what can I do?"

Bella stood by the stove, unable to take her eyes off him. She had always marveled at David's ability to move from one plane of feeling to the next without any apparent hangover. Her heart was still thumping loudly in her chest, and the questions she wanted to ask him were crowding her brain, begging to be released. Yet there he was, washed up and ready to be fed, as though it were no big deal to waltz back into her life after a two-month absence.

She had to smile though. Because he was there, and that fact, very simply, made her happy.

"Bella?"

"All right," she said. "I guess we need another place setting. There aren't going to be thirteen at the table after all."

He hung the towel up on the rack and came over to her. Taking her face in his hands, he kissed her lightly on the mouth. "We can talk later, okay? Now, where is the silverware?"

————◆————

It was a lively meal, filled with laughter and some arguing. What was amazing to Bella was how well her friends' husbands seem to take to David. Tony was a lawyer and T.R. was involved in music, yet the three of them seemed able to talk on a variety of subjects, from sports to politics, without there being any huge personality conflicts.

Kate's attitude toward David was warily subdued. Bella imagined her hot-tempered Irish friend wasn't quite ready to forgive him yet. Bella herself didn't know how she felt about that, or even what David wanted from her. But for now it was enough, she thought as she looked around at the happy, glowing faces, that he was in the country, in this city, in this room with her. It was enough.

People started leaving at ten, and the three youngsters, with liberal help from those who were left, tackled the kitchen. When the job was done, Sam and Dee announced that they were going off to hear a band, which made Kate and Bella look at each other with raised eyebrows.

Then Alex asked if he could borrow Bella's car, as he wanted to visit an old high school girlfriend.

Bella stood at the front door, waving to Kate and T.R., Hollis and Tony, as they got into their cars and drove off down the driveway. She stayed there for a moment, letting the crisp night air cool down her overheated face. Then she turned back into the house.

David was waiting for her, and they were finally alone.

TEN

Bella was extremely uncomfortable as she looked at David and, after the effusive good-byes she had bidden to her guests, aware of the quiet. "Sit down, won't you?" she said, taking refuge in politeness and feeling strangely shy in his presence.

"Would you like some coffee?" she asked. "Or some more pie?"

A smile twitched at his mouth. "Bella, I just had three cups of coffee, two pieces of pumpkin pie, and one of apple. The furthest thing from my mind right now is food."

"Oh."

So they sat there in the living room, seated across from each other on the oversize suede couches that fit the room's dimensions. One lamp and the steady, crackling fire in the fireplace provided soft lighting and the only sound in the room.

If she didn't count her heartbeat.

She glanced around the room, reminded suddenly of the time when she was decorating the house and had worried that she didn't know what she was doing and had turned to Jake for his opinion. He had said laughingly that she was the one with the class, not him, and he trusted her to make the right decisions.

She wondered why she was thinking about Jake just then, with David there in the room. Then she knew that she took refuge in her late husband's memory whenever her feelings about David were too turbulent.

"I feel so nervous now that you're here," she admitted, looking down at her clenched hands as they lay on her lap.

"Why are you nervous?"

"Because I don't know *why* you're here. I mean, I'm glad you are, but—"

"You want to know what's going on in my head," he said. "About you, about us."

"Something like that."

He expelled a quick breath, then favored her with one of his small half-smiles. "I have no pat answers. But here's what I do know. I'm miserable without you," he said. "I feel as if part of me is missing."

He delivered the words as a simple declarative statement, but Bella sensed all the emotions underneath—wonder, fear, and a little anger. The tears welled up, unbidden, and she wondered how she could possibly have any more left. "Oh, David, I feel the same way."

With a swift movement he rose and came over to where she was seated and kneeled in front of her, pulling her into his arms. He kissed her eyes and cheeks and along her hairline.

"Bella, Bella, Bella." He groaned, his warm breath against her ear.

Closing her eyes, she put her hands on his shoulders, feeling the soft cotton of his shirt under her fingertips and drinking in the litany of her name spoken softly by the man she loved.

"How I've missed you," he said, his mouth planting quick kisses on her neck and cheeks, settling finally on her lips. He ran his tongue over the moist skin inside her mouth, murmuring all the while, telling her how much he'd missed her, how special she was, how much a part of his life she had become.

Exhilaration flooded her; as suddenly as the tears had appeared, they disappeared, and she was on fire. Her body reacted passionately to David's onslaught, remembering past pleasures and readying itself for new ones. She opened her mouth to him, inviting his tongue inside, offering hers to taste, to tease, to dance.

She was wearing a loose silk hostess gown, and David reached down for the hem and pushed the garment up and over her head, letting it drape over the couch behind her. Still on his knees in front of her, he unhooked her bra, and eased it off her shoulder, kissing and tonguing the soft weight of her breasts. His fingertips teased her nipple into a tight peak of desire. Her very skin burned at his touch. She felt herself shuddering with need for him as his mouth caught one taut bud and licked and bit it till she cried out and grasped his head with her hands. Tension sang along the network of nerves that reached from her breasts to her womb, tightening like the strings of a violin.

"I remember how incredibly soft you are," he whispered, now teasing the other nipple as he eased his hand down to the apex of her thighs.

Through the thin wisp of lace, his fingertips stroked the moist folds of flesh there, and she felt a moan rising in her throat. He pulled this last barrier down and off, then eased her legs apart and kissed a trail of warmth along the tender flesh of her inner thighs. When she felt the wild, intimate heat of his mouth loving her, his tongue flicking back and forth over the small hard nub buried in her mound, she arched her back and cried out, "Oh, David!"

She fell back against the couch, shivering, her hips moving against the onslaught of his tongue and mouth and hands. There was another tactile impression, a new one, and she realized in the part of her mind that was still functioning that David's mustache and beard were rasping against her tender flesh, and that the soft bristles were almost—but not quite—painful, and extremely erotic.

She tangled her fingers in his thick, curly hair as she was bombarded with one sensation after another—hot blood coursed through her body, her breath sped up, her muscles tightened, till she knew she would die.

David was aggressive in his pleasuring of her, giving her no chance to breathe, to think, even to pleasure him. He drew her knees up so that her legs draped over his shoulders, granting him even more intimate access to her. His fingers parted her and he licked and tasted and loved her even more deeply, even more relentlessly. All she could do was go where he was directing her to go—to the edge of the world, and then over.

Her head twisted from side to side, and she was aware of his own ragged breaths mingling with hers, and then she went up in flames, her body doing a mindless dance of long-drawn-out ecstasy so intense that it tore her apart in great shuddering bursts that seemed to splinter all the parts of her, tossing them into eternity.

In the moments afterward, when she began to journey back to the present and her body's rhythms slowed down, he joined her on the couch, pulling her into his arms and caressing her hair and her back with slow, soothing strokes.

At one point Bella murmured huskily, "Did we

have an earthquake? I distinctly felt the earth move."

"So did I," he said.

"But it couldn't have for you," she said, reaching for him. "Let me—"

He stilled her hand. "Not now, Bella. Later. There'll be plenty of time later."

He lifted her hostess robe and eased it back over her head, the smooth silk feeling cool against her skin. She snuggled against him. "Mmm. Later."

She sat up abruptly and put her hand over her mouth. "My God. The boys! I completely forgot about them. Can you believe it? What if they had walked in here and seen me sprawled out here on the couch? What if they'd seen you doing what you were doing? Oh, no."

David chuckled. "They just left, remember? It will be hours before they get home."

"I guess so." She leaned against him once again, closing her eyes, enjoying the feel of his strong hands as they continued to massage her gently.

"Do they know about me?" he asked.

Angling her head, she looked up and met his eyes with directness. "What should they know?"

He nodded. "You're right. I want to talk about that." He brought her body around so that she was facing him on the couch, then took her hands and held them between his. "I've spent a lot of time alone, thinking. And I keep remembering your face when you sat in the guest house and asked me if I would be willing to try to love you. I am willing, but I can't promise anything."

Lifting her hands up to his mouth, he kissed the knuckles, then sighed. "I'm flawed, Bella," he went on. "This whole love thing doesn't come easily to me. Besides, I'm not even sure I believe in the kind of love you talk about. I've been alone for so long, and I was so sure I would always be alone."

With a bleak smile he said, "I'm not sure if this is enough for you, but it's the best I can do right now. I want to try. You are too special, too wonderful, you mean too much to me to let you out of my life."

She was overcome, not for the first or even the second time, with the desolation behind David's words. She wanted so badly to make it all right for him. She reached up and smoothed his beard with her fingertips, meeting his gaze and smiling. "David," she began.

A sudden fear gripped her. How would he react to her news? She had to tell him, of course, but she had a strong sense that it would ruin the nice, close moment they were sharing. Or, she thought with a sudden flare of hope, in the spirit of trying to escape old demons, maybe he would accept the news with equanimity, even calm.

She swallowed, willing herself to plunge right in. "David, I have some news for you, something that will change both our lives. I . . . I went to the doctor."

"Is something wrong? Are you ill?" There was concern in his eyes.

"No, no, far from it." She stroked his cheek again, the hair of his beard wiry and soft at the same time against her palm. "The thing is, I'm going to have a baby."

She watched his face carefully for his reaction, but he seemed only puzzled. "You mean you're adopting?"

"No. I'm . . . pregnant."

Disbelief registered in the narrowing of his eyes. "Are you sure?"

"Yes."

"Maybe it's—what do they call them?—a hysterical pregnancy. I know how much you wish you'd had more kids."

She smiled. "The only thing hysterical about it was my reaction. Hysterical joy."

As her words sank in, his mouth set in a hard line, his pale green eyes glittered with anger. "Whose is it?"

"David!"

"Well? Obviously you've been with someone else."

Probably she'd been naive, but she hadn't expected this at all. "David!" she said again. "It's yours."

"No way."

"But it is. I promise it is."

"It can't be. Remember? I had a vasectomy."

She held her hands out, palms up. "I don't know how these things work. It must not have taken, or something like that."

His grim mouth tightened. "It was over ten years ago. In all that time I've never gotten anyone pregnant. I think it took pretty well."

Finally, for the second time that night, the anger surged up from somewhere deep inside. She was being insulted, doubted, by the man who, not two minutes ago, had been willing to try to turn his life around because of how much he needed her, the man who, moments before that, had gifted her with the most intimate act of love possible between a man and a woman.

Bella could feel her posture stiffening with rage. "I don't know about all those other women you've been with," she said. "What I do know about is *me, my* body, which is at this moment carrying *your* child."

He didn't answer her, but his nostrils flared and mistrust blazed from his eyes like an unfriendly beacon.

"How dare you?" Bella said, her teeth tight against each other. "How dare you do this to me?"

"How dare I do this to you?" he shot back. "What the hell do you think you're doing to me?"

She stared at him in angry despair. "You're doubting my word. You don't trust me. I tell you we're going to have a baby, and you accuse me of sleeping with someone else and trying to pass it off as yours. That's despicable! If you know me at all, you know I would never do that. If you cared about me at all, the way you say you do, it wouldn't even cross your mind."

In a fury she vaulted off the couch. "Get out!" When he didn't move, she strode to the front door, wrenching it open.

She turned and watched him coming toward her, his face stern and hard. She felt a moment of fear, but refused to acknowledge it. "Get out," she said again.

He stood, a fierce giant towering over her, and she could see him warring with himself as he struggled to give her the benefit of the doubt. "Bella, look—"

"No. I refuse to be reasonable, I refuse to be understanding. Go away, David. Get out of here. Now."

Pain, cold and dark, flashed for an instant in his eyes. Then he said, "All right!" and stormed out the door, slamming it behind him.

David stood at the door of the old brownstone, hesitating before pushing the intercom button. Did he really want to do this? he asked himself, and he turned and looked longingly at the busy Cambridge street. Students on bikes, books tucked in the front basket. An old man slowly making his way down the street with the aid of a walker. Two young lovers, holding hands and unable to take their eyes off each other.

His mouth tightened as he remembered. That feeling could have been his, but he'd blown it. He'd walked out of Bella's house and gone into the mountains, unreachable, alone. And there, he'd let all the memories—childhood and on—flood through him, all the pain he'd kept himself from feeling. It had been a period of mourning for something he'd never had, and at the end of it, he'd come home to Cambridge.

His first stop had been at the office of the urologist who had performed the vasectomy. There he'd found out what a fool he'd been.

David leaned against the brown brick wall of the old building, his eyes closed, and pictured Bella's face at that moment when he'd hurt her so deeply, he doubted she'd forgive him. A fool, he called himself again. A damned, stupid fool.

Outside the doctor's office, he'd wanted to get right on the phone and apologize. But then he'd asked himself, And then what? Propose marriage? Be a father? Move into Bella's house and become part of her life? Could he do that? Was it even remotely possible, given the cutoff, detached, singular man he was?

Almost without conscious awareness he'd made his way to this familiar building. He used to dread coming here. Somehow, today, the dread wasn't there. Instead, he experienced a sensation that felt like ice melting at the core of his soul.

He pushed the button and after a few moments, his mother's voice came over the intercom. "Yes?"

"It's David."

"David?" He could hear surprise in her tone. "Come right up."

She opened the door to the apartment, that faintly mocking smile of hers in place. But for some reason he saw past the smile to the worried look in her eyes.

"David? Are you all right?" she asked, pulling him into the room.

"That's open to interpretation."

He gave her a hug. It was awkward. They'd never been physically affectionate with each other. But he wanted to try, and after a moment he felt her relax a little against him and return the hug.

His father appeared in the doorway of the room that served as his study, holding his glasses in his hand. He looked tired, older. He rubbed his eyes, as though they were strained, then put his glasses on.

"David," he said, obviously pleased. His father had always been easier for him to deal with. "How nice to see you. What brings you to Cambridge?"

David felt as if he were seeing both his parents for

the first time. Good people, well-meaning, caught up in their academic world, not demonstrative, uncomfortable with affection, uncomfortable with emotions. Like him.

But good people nevertheless.

He took a deep breath. "I guess I need some answers."

His father's eyebrows rose, and a quick, silent look passed between him and his wife. Then the older man smiled. "Can we know the questions first?"

David smiled back. This was what he needed to do, it was clear, before he saw Bella again. Clear away some past wreckage. Until he did, he would be no good to her or to their unborn child.

Bella lit the first night's candle on the menorah and said the brief prayer silently. Then she turned around and smiled at all her friends. "There," she said. "Happy Hanukkah."

Tonight was the annual Hanukkah-Christmas party that she threw for everyone who worked at Annabella and Annabella Deux and their families. The house was decorated with holly and mistletoe, and a blue and white streamer over the fireplace read HAPPY HOLIDAYS TO ALL. Kate passed around a tray of Hanukkah cookies, while Sam and Alex distributed dreidels—four-sided miniature tops—to all the children.

The living room was bustling with activity. Hollis had organized some Victorian games for the older children; Dee played on the floor with an adorable four-year-old girl; T.R. and Tony stood by the punch bowl, making sure the eggnog held out. People sang songs and laughed. It would go on for hours, as it did every year, culminating in the opening of presents. Bella's gift to her staff, in addition to their regular bonus, was a generous gift certificate to a large supermarket. Things had been tight for everyone this year.

The boys had been home for several days, but Bella had hardly seen them, they were so busy with their friends. She was determined to tell them her news before making the public announcement at the party, and it would have to be now. She was a little concerned about how they would take it, but it had to be done.

"Hollis," she said. "Will you stand in for me for a few moments?"

"Of course, Bella." Hollis smiled warmly. "What are partners for?"

"Sam," Bella said, "could I see you a minute in the kitchen?"

"Uh-oh," Alex said to his brother. "That usually means we did something wrong. Did you forget to fill the tank again?"

"You too, Alex." Bella tried to keep the nervousness out of her voice.

"You must have forgotten to take out the garbage," Sam said to Alex.

"Neither of you forgot anything. Come on."

Once she had them seated at the table, she had a hard time starting. Her discomfort must have shown on her face, because Alex, who always read her easily, said, "Mom, what's wrong?"

She smiled. "Nothing's wrong. It's just that there's going to be a change around here, and I'm not quite sure how to tell you both."

"Are we moving?"

"No, nothing like that. I—" She automatically pressed her hand against her subtly rounded stomach. The new life inside gave her courage. "I'm pregnant."

Both their mouths fell open, and she fought down the urge to laugh at the picture of amazement they represented. From the front of the house she heard the doorbell ring, then sounds of laughter and shouts of "Happy Holidays," as a new guest was ushered into the living room.

Sam was the first to find his voice. "You're pregnant?"

"Yes. You're going to have a little brother or sister. In June. Maybe by the time school's finished. And I'm very happy about it," she added firmly.

"But who—?" Sam asked.

"David, of course," his brother said matter-of-factly.

"David? But he—" Sam didn't finish his sentence. He just shook his head. "Wow, Mom."

They sat, the three of them, at the same table that over the years had been the scene of food fights, snickering, taunting each other about Little League hits and misses, then pimples, then girls . . .

"Wow," Sam said again after a while.

"Do you mind?" she asked, hoping her question didn't sound too tremulous.

"Mind?" Alex's smile was broad. "I think it's great. It's kind of weird thinking of your mother, you know—as a woman. I mean—"

"I think I know what you mean," she said wryly.

"What's going on with David?" Sam wanted to know. "I thought you said you hadn't seen him in a while."

Alex cut in. "Is he dumping you or anything because of this?" He looked stern, ready to leap to her defense. She wanted to hug him till he dropped.

"No. It was my decision. And I don't think I want to discuss David with you. I wanted you to know about it, that's all, and tell you both that I love you very much."

They looked at each other, her two no-longer-children, then back at her and nodded. She heard the doorbell ring again and she rose, feeling that she'd left her party too long.

"If there's anything we can do . . ." Sam said, rising from his chair.

"Same here," Alex added. "I don't know what, really, but anything . . ."

"You already have, by taking it so well. You've both grown into men that I like knowing. I'm so proud of you."

"Stop, Mom," Sam said. "You're embarrassing us."

She laughed. "What else is new?"

They grinned back. She put a hand through each son's bent arm, and the three of them walked out of the kitchen, down the hallway, and into the living room.

David was there.

David, looking incongruous with two large shopping bags by his side, his hair neatly trimmed, his beard gone, and wearing a tweed jacket. The only Davidlike consistency in his appearance was the fact that he wore jeans. But they looked new. David looked new—rested and healthy. There was a lack of tension in his face as he smiled at her.

Her heart fluttered in her chest. He looked wonderful.

"Hello, Bella," David said softly, drinking in the sight of her. She glowed with life, not just the life she was carrying, but that natural, spontaneous happiness of hers that swooped up everything and everyone in her path and infused them with joy.

Without taking his eyes off her, David said, "Hi, Sam, Alex. How've you been?"

The boys nodded, and Sam said, "Fine," but they remained at Bella's side, as if not sure what to do, how to react to him. He understood. In their eyes he had deserted their mother and their loyalty was with her. They glanced over at Bella for guidance, but she seemed unable to take her eyes off him either.

"Hello, David," she said, her voice husky with emotion. "Happy Hanukkah."

He smiled and nodded. "Happy Hanukkah to you too."

Kate came up and stood next to David, looked from him to Bella and back again, then picked up one of the shopping bags. Peering inside, she announced, "Presents. Lots of them."

"For Bella and the boys," David said.

"Really?" Sam said.

"Thanks," Alex joined in, looking pleased. Then he darted another look at his mother as if to ask if his reaction was all right. She smiled reassuringly.

Hollis appeared at David's other side and grasped the handles of the other bag. "We're putting all the gifts near the fireplace and opening them later. Okay with you?"

"Okay with you?" David repeated, but directed the question to Bella. "I'd like to stay. I'd like to stay very much."

The moment hung in time, only a few heartbeats in length, but in that short interval, unspoken questions and answers and declarations went back and forth between them, too quickly to be measured, and too private for anyone to hear except for David and the woman he watched as though his life were in the balance.

Bella felt her entire body soften as the subtle strain she'd been under since David had left three weeks before drained out of her. "Okay with me."

Walking up to her, he held out his hand and she took it. He turned them so they were walking down the hallway, back toward the kitchen. "We'll be a few minutes," David said, looking back over his shoulder, and was rewarded by an approving smile from Hollis and the thumbs-up sign from Kate. Draping an arm around Bella's shoulder, he pulled her to him and was gratified to feel her arm encircling his waist, her head leaning against his chest as they walked.

"Why the kitchen?" she said.

"I didn't think you'd want your guests to see you being waltzed into your bedroom."

She laughed softly.

Inside the door, he backed her up against the wall and turned his body so it leaned into hers. Then he kissed her with all the pent-up feeling that had been in him for weeks. He was elated by the way her lips parted to grant him access to her, by the way her arms found their way around his neck, her hands raking through his hair, her body molded to his as though she, too, couldn't tolerate the thought of separateness.

Finally, he broke the kiss. Leaning his elbows against the wall on either side of her head, he gazed into her eyes. They were warm, accepting, forgiving. Bella would always accept him and forgive him, he knew that. It was her nature.

Even so, he had to say it. "I'm sorry."

He sifted a few loose strands of her ebony hair through his fingers, his eyes roaming all over her wonderful face, taking in all the wonderful components that made it so special to him.

"I'm so sorry," he went on, "that I doubted you. It was wrong, terribly wrong. And I'm sorry that I ran away from you. I think I did it out of sheer terror. You made me feel all these feelings that I wasn't used to. And I'm sorry for all the years I've run away from myself. Except if I hadn't, I might never have met you. And that would have caused me the most sorrow of all."

Her lashes lowered, and he felt the shudder that passed through her body.

"Bella," he asked. "Are you all right?"

"I thought I had lost you. And I didn't know what I could do about it. And now you're here, and I'm afraid I'm dreaming."

He put his hands on the back of her head and eased her face into his neck, stroking the cool black silk of her hair. "It's no dream. I'm here. And—"

He paused, swallowed, then said, "I love you." His hands stopped their stroking movement. "Amazing. I didn't die."

Bella tilted her head back. "What?"

"I've never said that before. To anyone. I had no idea what to expect. I love you," he said again. "I love you and I want to be a father to our child."

She gazed at him with simple directness. "And you're sure now it is our child?"

"I went back to the doctor who performed the original tying-off."

As he talked, he hugged her to him and walked them over to the table. They both sat where they usually sat, across from each other under the lamp's soft glow.

"Apparently," he explained, "I was supposed to go for a follow-up after six months, but I must have been down a hole somewhere on the other side of the world, and never got around to it." His mouth twisted with amusement. "There is still what they euphemistically call a slight leak."

"Did you have the, uh, leak taken care of?"

"No. I wanted to talk it over with you first. I mean, we may want more."

"We may? I think I'd better have this one first."

He shrugged. "Well, I didn't know. We have a while to make up our minds."

We. He kept saying we. David was talking about their future now, like a man who had no doubts about commitment at all. David? This was David? Bella wanted the world to stop for a moment so she could savor it.

He picked up one of her hands and played absently with the fingers. "I've done a lot of thinking. I went back and saw my folks. Told them about you. Talked about what went on when I was a kid. Nothing got fixed, of course. That doesn't happen overnight. But I came away from them thinking that we might talk some more, the three of us, once in a while, and try to repair the estrangement. My mother had tears in her eyes when I said good-bye."

"I know from personal experience that when a mother has tears in her eyes, that's a good sign."

"And so, the thing is, I'd like you to marry me."

Her mouth dropped open, and she stared at him. "You what?"

He stopped playing with her fingers and looked up at her with a rueful grin. "I'm proposing, Bella. I love you, and we're going to have a child, and I'm asking you to marry me. What do you say?"

"As Sam likes to say, wow. You don't do anything halfway, do you?"

"What do you think?" he persisted.

She thought about it for a moment, then shook her head, still reeling from the suddenness of his proposal. "But marriage means commitment and complications and sometimes being invaded. And you're such a solitary kind of man."

"I know."

"And I'm older than you and have grown kids."

"The first is insignificant and the second means we have baby-sitters. What else?"

"And you travel all the time."

"I'll travel less of the time now, especially if I have you to come home to. I'd already come to that conclusion anyway. It's time to put down some roots, maybe finish my Ph.D., teach some seminars. I have offers from a couple of universities."

"We'd have to move? I'd have to leave my house?"

"We don't have to do anything, Bella," he said gently. "I just thought . . . maybe this house has a lot of memories for you, and it might be good to start over in a place where we can build our own memories." He shrugged. "Or maybe we don't have to move. We'll work it out."

She considered his words, and the meaning behind them, and she knew they were true. It was time to put Jake away. He had been the love of her youth. David was the love of the rest of her life. "You're right, of course," she said. "If we did marry, I couldn't expect you to fit into my life, could I? That would be pretty selfish of me."

He smiled, but his eyes said he was waiting. "*If* we did marry . . . ?"

"I'm not being coy, David," she said. "I think I'm still digesting all this."

"Are you punishing me? I guess I couldn't blame you."

"No, not at all," she said, putting her hand on his arm. "It's just that you're so different, so . . . determined, so definite. I'm not used to this David."

"Then maybe you don't love me?"

"Oh, no, no. I love you terribly."

"Good." He emitted a relieved sigh. "Then what's the problem?"

She looked down at the fine gold hair on his wrist and smiled wryly. "I guess there isn't one. I'm kind of overwhelmed, that's all. But seriously, we're such opposites. Don't you think that might be a problem? What if I drive you crazy? I cluck over people I love, David. Ask the boys, they'll tell you."

He nodded, the corners of his mouth turning up with one of his half-smiles. "Yeah, you do cluck."

"And I'll worry about you when you go away. And I'll keep offering to feed you. And I'm not sure how much I can change. Won't that drive you up a wall?"

"Maybe. And sometimes I need time alone, and I have trouble talking about feelings. And sometimes I get too carried away with my work. We're each going to have to practice a little tolerance, I guess. Besides, I have a confession to make." His smile was tinged with embarrassment. "I like it when you cluck over me. It makes me feel cared for."

She looked at him with wonder. "Well, of course you're cared for. That's exactly why I do it."

His face was suddenly serious as he put his hand over hers and gripped it tightly. "Bella, I want a family. Our child. Your kids. You. You are my family."

"Family," she repeated.

At that moment, the flower that was her love for him, that had been slowly unfolding, seeking the light during this whole conversation, finally stretched and expanded into full bloom. Oh, yes, she loved this man, with every living, breathing part of her. All the rest was . . . details.

Bella stroked David's cheek and looked lovingly into his eyes. "Family," she said again. "You said the magic word. Of course I'll marry you."

He looked unbelieving for a moment, then his face broke out into the biggest, most generous, most beautiful smile she'd ever seen. He pushed himself up from the table and offered his hand to her. "Let's do it," he said.

She gave him her hand and got up too. "Do what?"

"Go out there and make the announcement. Which would you prefer first—the baby or the marriage?"

"Oh, dear," Bella sighed. "Times really have changed, haven't they?"

THE EDITOR'S CORNER

There's never too much of a good thing when it comes to romances inspired by beloved stories, so next month we present TREASURED TALES II. Coming your way are six brand-new LOVESWEPTs written by some of the most talented authors of romantic fiction today. You'll delight in their contemporary versions of age-old classics . . . and experience the excitement and passion of falling in love. TREASURED TALES II— what a way to begin the new year!

The first book in our fabulous line up is **PERFECT DOUBLE** by Cindy Gerard, LOVESWEPT #660. In this wonderful retelling of *The Prince and the Pauper* business mogul Logan Prince gets saved by a stranger from a near-fatal mugging, then wakes up in an unfamiliar bed to find a reluctant angel with a siren's body bandaging his wounds! Logan vows to win Carmen Sanchez's heart—

even if it means making a daring bargain with his look-alike rescuer and trading places with the cowboy drifter. It take plenty of wooing before Carmen surrenders to desire—and even more sweet persuasion to regain her trust once he confesses to his charade. A top-notch story from talented Cindy.

Homer's epic poem *The Odyssey* has never been as romantic as Billie Green's version, **BABY, COME BACK**, LOVESWEPT #661. Like Odysseus, David Moore has spent a long time away from home. Finally free after six years in captivity, and with an unrecognizable face and voice, he's not sure if there's still room for him in the lives of his sweet wife, Kathy, and their son, Ben. When he returns home, he masquerades as a handyman, determined to be close to his son, aching to show his wife that, though she's now a successful businesswoman, she still needs him. Poignant and passionate, this love story shows Billie at her finest!

Tom Falconson lives the nightmare of *The Invisible Man* in Terry Lawrence's **THE SHADOW LOVER**, LOVESWEPT #662. When a government experiment goes awry and renders the dashingly virile intelligence agent invisible, Tom knows he has only one person to turn to. Delighted by mysteries, ever in search of the unexplained, Alice Willow opens her door to him, offering him refuge and the sensual freedom to pull her dangerously close. But even as Tom sets out to show her that the phantom in her arms is a flesh-and-blood man, he wonders if their love is strong enough to prove that nothing is impossible. Terry provides plenty of thrills and tempestuous emotions in this fabulous tale.

In Jan Hudson's **FLY WITH ME**, LOVESWEPT #663, Sawyer Hayes is a modern-day Peter Pan who soars through the air in a gleaming helicopter. He touches down in Pip LeBaron's backyard with an offer of a job in his company, but the computer genius quickly informs him that for now she's doing nothing except making up for the childhood she missed. Bewitched by her delicate beauty, Sawyer decides to help her, though her kissable mouth persuades him that a few grown-up games would be more fun. Pip soon welcomes his tantalizing embrace, turning to liquid moonlight beneath his touch. But is there a future together for a man who seems to live for fun and a lady whose work has been her whole life? Jan weaves her magic in this enchanting romance.

"The Ugly Duckling" was Linda Cajio's inspiration for her new LOVESWEPT, **HE'S SO SHY,** #664—and if there ever was an ugly duckling, Richard Creighton was it. Once a skinny nerd with glasses, he's now impossibly sexy, irresistibly gorgeous, and the hottest actor on the big screen. Penelope Marsh can't believe that this leading man in her cousin's movie is the same person she went to grade school with. She thinks he's definitely out of her league, but Richard doesn't agree. Drawn to the willowy schoolteacher, Richard dares her to accept what's written in the stars—that she's destined to be his leading lady for life. Linda delivers a surefire hit.

Last, but certainly not least, is **ANIMAL MAGNETISM** by Bonnie Pega, LOVESWEPT #665. Only Dr. Dolittle is Sebastian Kent's equal when it comes to relating to animals—but Danni Sullivan insists the veterinarian still needs her help. After all, he's new in her hometown, and no one knows every cat, bull, and pig there as well as she. For once giving in to impulse, Sebastian hires her on the spot—then thinks twice about it when her touch arouses long-denied yearnings. He can charm any beast, but he definitely needs a lesson in how to soothe his wounded heart. And Danni has just the right touch to heal his pain—and make him believe in love once more. Bonnie will delight you with this thoroughly enchanting story.

Happy reading!

With warmest wishes,

Nita Taublib

Nita Taublib

Associate Publisher

P.S. Don't miss the fabulous women's fiction Bantam has coming in January: **DESIRE**, the newest novel from bestselling author Amanda Quick; **LONG TIME COMING,** Sandra Brown's classic contemporary romance; **STRANGER IN MY ARMS** by R. J. Kaiser, a novel of romantic suspense in which a woman who has lost her memory is in danger of also losing her life; and **WHERE DOLPHINS GO** by LOVESWEPT author Peggy Webb, a truly unique romance that integrates into its story the fascinating ability of dolphins to aid injured children. We'll be giving you a sneak peek at these wonderful books in next month's LOVESWEPTs. And immediately following this page, look for a preview of the exciting women's novels from Bantam that are *available now!*

Don't miss these exciting books by your
favorite Bantam authors

On sale in November:

ADAM'S FALL
by *Sandra Brown*

NOTORIOUS
by *Patricia Potter*

*PRINCESS OF
THIEVES*
by *Katherine O'Neal*

*CAPTURE THE
NIGHT*
by *Geralyn Dawson*

And in hardcover from Doubleday
ON WINGS OF MAGIC
by *Kay Hooper*

Adam's Fall

Available this month in hardcover
from *New York Times*
bestselling author

SANDRA BROWN

Over the past few years, Lilah Mason had watched
her sister Elizabeth find love, get married, and have
children, while she's been more than content to
channel her energies into a career. A physical thera-
pist with an unsinkable spirit and unwavering compassion, she's one of the best in the field. But
when Lilah takes on a demanding new case, her
patient's life isn't the only one transformed. She's
never had a tougher patient than Adam, who challenges her methods and authority at every turn. Yet
Lilah is determined to help him recover the life he's
lost. What she can't see is that while she's winning
Adam's battle, she's losing her heart. Now, as pro-
fessional duty and passionate yearnings clash, Lilah
must choose the right course for them both.

*Sizzling Romance from One of the
World's Hottest Pens*

Patricia Potter

Nationally bestselling author of
Renegade and **Lightning**

NOTORIOUS

*The owner of the most popular saloon in San Francisco,
Catalina Hilliard knows Marsh Canton is trouble the
moment she first sees him. He's not the first to attempt to
open a rival saloon next door to the Silver Slipper, but he
does possess a steely strength that was missing from the
men she'd driven out of business. Even more perilous to
Cat's plans is the spark of desire that flares between
them, a desire that's about to spin her carefully orchestrated life out of control . . .*

"We have nothing to discuss," she said coldly,
even as she struggled to keep from trembling. All
her thoughts were in disarray. He was so adept at
personal invasion. That look in his eyes of pure radiance, of physical need, almost burned through her.

Fifteen years. Nearly fifteen years since a man
had touched her so intimately. And he was doing
it only with his eyes!

And, dear Lucifer, she was responding.

She'd thought herself immune from desire. If
she'd ever had any, she believed it had been killed

long ago by brutality and shame and utter abhorrence of an act that gave men power and left her little more than a thing to be used and hurt. She'd never felt this bubbling, boiling warmth inside, this craving that was more than physical hunger.

That's what frightened her most of all.

But she wouldn't show it. She would never show it! She didn't even like Canton, devil take him. She didn't like anything about him. And she would send him back to wherever he came. Tail between his legs. No matter what it took. And she would never feel desire again.

But now she had little choice, unless she wished to stand here all afternoon, his hand burning a brand into her. He wasn't going to let her go, and perhaps it was time to lay her cards on the table. She preferred open warfare to guerrilla fighting. She hadn't felt right about the kidnapping and beating—even if she did frequently regret her moment of mercy on his behalf.

She shrugged and his hand relaxed slightly. They left, and he flagged down a carriage for hire. Using those strangely elegant manners that still puzzled her, he helped her inside with a grace that would put royalty to shame.

He left her then for a moment and spoke to the driver, passing a few bills up to him, then returned and vaulted to the seat next to her. Hard-muscled thigh pushed against her leg; his tanned arm, made visible by the rolled-up sleeve, touched her much smaller one, the wiry male hair brushing against her skin, sparking a thousand tiny charges. His scent, a spicy mixture of bay and soap, teased her senses. Everything about him—the strength and power and raw masculinity that he made no attempt to conceal—made her feel fragile, delicate.

But not vulnerable, she told herself. Never vulnerable again. She would fight back by seizing control and keeping it.

She straightened her back and smiled. A seductive smile. A smile that had entranced men for the last ten years. A practiced smile that knew exactly how far to go. A kind of promise that left doors opened, while permitting retreat. It was a smile that kept men coming to the Silver Slipper even as they understood they had no real chance of realizing the dream.

Canton raised an eyebrow. "You *are* very good," he said admiringly.

She shrugged. "It usually works."

"I imagine it does," he said. "Although I doubt if most of the men you use it on have seen the thornier part of you."

"Most don't irritate me as you do."

"Irritate, Miss Cat?"

"Don't call me Cat. My name is Catalina."

"Is it?"

"Is yours really Taylor Canton?"

The last two questions were spoken softly, dangerously, both trying to probe weaknesses, and both recognizing the tactic of the other.

"I would swear to it on a Bible," Marsh said, his mouth quirking.

"I'm surprised you have one, or know what one is."

"I had a very good upbringing, Miss Cat." He emphasized the last word.

"And then what happened?" she asked caustically.

The sardonic amusement in his eyes faded. "A great deal. And what is your story?"

Dear God, his voice was mesmerizing, an intimate song that said nothing but wanted everything. Low and deep and provocative. Compelling. And irresistible . . . almost.

"I had a very poor upbringing," she said. "And then a great deal happened."

For the first time since she'd met him, she saw real humor in his eyes. Not just that cynical amusement as if he were some higher being looking down on a world inhabited by silly children. "You're the first woman I've met with fewer scruples than my own," he said, admiration again in his voice.

She opened her eyes wide. "You have some?"

"As I told you that first night, I don't usually mistreat women."

"Usually?"

"Unless provoked."

"A threat, Mr. Canton?"

"I never threaten, Miss Cat. Neither do I turn down challenges."

"And you usually win?"

"Not usually, Miss Cat. Always." The word was flat. Almost ugly in its surety.

"So do I," she said complacently.

Their voices, Cat knew, had lowered into little more than husky whispers. The air in the closed carriage was sparking, hissing, crackling. Threatening to ignite. His hand moved to her arm, his fingers running up and down it in slow, caressingly sensuous trails.

And then the heat surrounding them was as intense as that in the heart of a volcano. Intense and violent. She wondered very briefly if this was a version of hell. She had just decided it was when he bent toward her, his lips brushing over hers.

And heaven and hell collided.

PRINCESS OF THIEVES
by
Katherine O'Neal

"A brilliant new talent bound to
make her mark on the genre."
—Iris Johansen

*Mace Blackwood is the greatest con artist in the world,
a demon whose family is responsible for the death of
Saranda Sherwin's parents. And though he might be
luring her to damnation itself, Saranda allows herself to be set aflame by the fire in his dark eyes. It's a
calculated surrender that he finds both intoxicating
and infuriating, for one evening alone with the
blue-eyed siren can never be enough. And now he
will stop at nothing to have her forever. . . .*

Saranda could read his intentions in the gleam
of his midnight eyes. "Stay away from me," she
gasped.

"Surely, you're not afraid of me? I've already
admitted defeat."

"As if I'd trust anything you'd say."

Mace raised a brow. "Trust? No, sweetheart, it's
not about trust between us."

"You're right. It's about a battle between our
families that has finally come to an end. The

Sherwins have won, Blackwood. You have no further hand to play."

Even as she said it, she knew it wasn't true. Despite the bad blood between them, they had unfinished business. Because the game, this time, had gone too far.

"That's separate. The feud, the competition—that has nothing to do with what's happening between you and me."

"You must think I'm the rankest kind of amateur. Do you think I don't know what you're up to?"

He put his hand to her cheek and stroked the softly shadowed contours of her face. "What am I up to?"

He was so close, she could feel the muscles of his chest toying with her breasts. Against all sense, she hungered to be touched.

"If you can succeed in seducing me, you can run to Winston with the news—"

His hand drifted from her cheek down the naked column of her neck, to softly caress the slope of her naked shoulder. "I could tell him you slept with me whether you do or not. But you know as well as I do he wouldn't believe me."

"That argument won't work either, Blackwood," she said in a dangerously breathy tone.

"Very well, Miss Sherwin. Why don't we just lay our cards on the table?"

"Why not indeed?"

"Then here it is. I don't like you any more than you like me. In fact, I can't think of a woman I'd be less likely to covet. My family cared for yours no more than yours cared for mine. But I find myself in the unfortunate circumstance of wanting you to distraction. For some reason I can't even fathom, I can't look at you without wondering what you'd look like panting in my arms. Without wanting to feel your naked skin beneath my hands. Or taste your sweat on my tongue. Without needing to come inside you and make you cry out in passion and lose some of that *goddamned* control." A faint moan escaped her throat. "You're all I think about. You're like a fever in my brain. I keep thinking if I took you *just once*, I might finally expel you from my mind. So I don't suppose either of us is leaving this office before we've had what you came for."

"I came to tell you—"

"You could have done that any time. You could have left me wondering for the rest of the night if the wedding would take place. But you didn't wait. You knew if this was going to happen, it had to be tonight. Because once you're Winston's wife, I won't come near you. The minute you say 'I do,' you and I take off the gloves, darling, and the real battle begins. So it's now or never." He lowered his mouth to her shoulder, and her breath left her in a sigh.

"Now or never," she repeated in a daze.

"One night to forget who we are and what it all means. You're so confident of winning. Surely, you wouldn't deny me the spoils of the game. Or more to the point . . . deny yourself."

She looked up and met his sweltering gaze. After three days of not seeing him, she'd forgotten how devastatingly handsome he was. "I shan't fall in love with you, if that's what you're thinking. This will give you no advantage over me. I'm still going after you with both barrels loaded."

"Stop trying so hard to figure it out. I don't give a hang what you think of me. And I don't need your tender mercy. I tell you point-blank, if you think you've won, you may be in for a surprise. But that's beside the point." He wrapped a curl around his finger. Then, taking the pins from her hair, one by one, he dropped them to the floor. She felt her taut nerves jump as each pin clicked against the tile.

He ran both hands through the silvery hair, fluffing it with his fingers, dragging them slowly through the length as he watched the play of light on the silky strands. It spilled like moonlight over her shoulders. "Did you have to be so beautiful?" he rasped.

"Do you have to look so much like a Blackwood?"

He looked at her for a moment, his eyes piercing hers, his hands tangled in her hair. "Tell me what you want."

She couldn't look at him. It brought back memories of his brother she'd rather not relive. As it was, she couldn't believe she was doing this. But she had to have him. It was as elemental as food for her body and air to breathe. Her eyes dropped to his mouth—that blatant, sexual mouth that could make her wild with a grin or wet with a word.

She closed her eyes. If she didn't look at him, maybe she could separate this moment from the past. From what his brother had done. Her voice was a mere whisper when she spoke. "I want you to stop wasting time," she told him, "and make love to me."

He let go of her hair and took her naked shoulders in his hands. Bending her backward, he brought his mouth to hers with a kiss so searing, it scalded her heart.

CAPTURE THE NIGHT

by Geralyn Dawson

Award-winning author of

The Texan's Bride

"My highest praise goes to this author
and her work, one of the best . . . I have
read in years."
—*Rendezvous*

*A desperate French beauty, the ruggedly handsome Texan
who rescues her, and their precious stolen "Rose" are swept
together by destiny as they each try to escape the secrets of
their past.*

Madeline groaned as the man called Sinclair saun-
tered toward her. This is all I need, she thought.

He stopped beside her and dipped into a perfect
imitation of a gentleman's bow. Eyes shining, he
looked up and said in his deplorable French, "Mad-
ame, do you by chance speak English? Apparently,
we'll be sharing a spot in line. I beg to make your
acquaintance."

She didn't answer.

He sighed and straightened. Then a wicked grin creased his face and in English he drawled, "Brazos Sinclair's my name, Texas born and bred. Most of my friends call me Sin, especially my lady friends. Nobody calls me Claire but once. I'll be sailin' with you on the *Uriel*."

Madeline ignored him.

Evidently, that bothered him not at all. "Cute baby," he said, peeking past the blanket. "Best keep him covered good though. This weather'll chill him."

Madeline bristled at the implied criticism. She glared at the man named Sin.

His grin faded. "Sure you don't speak English?"

She held her silence.

"Guess not, huh. That's all right, I'll enjoy conversin' with you anyway." He shot a piercing glare toward Victor Considérant, the colonists' leader and the man who had refused him a place on the *Uriel*. "I need a diversion, you see. Otherwise I'm liable to do something I shouldn't." Angling his head, he gave her another sweeping gaze. "You're a right fine lookin' woman, ma'am, a real beauty. Don't know that I think much of your husband, though, leavin' you here on the docks by your lonesome."

He paused and looked around, his stare snagging on a pair of scruffy sailors. "It's a dangerous thing for women to be alone in such a place, and for a beautiful one like you, well, I hesitate to think."

Obviously, Madeline said to herself.

The Texan continued, glancing around at the people milling along the wharf. " 'Course, I can't say I understand you Europeans. I've been here goin' on two years, and I'm no closer to figurin' y'all out now than I was the day I rolled off the boat." He reached into his jacket pocket and pulled out a pair of peppermint sticks.

Madeline declined the offer by shaking her head, and he returned one to his pocket before taking a slow lick of the second. "One thing, there's all those kings and royals. I think it's nothin' short of silly to climb on a high horse simply because blood family's been plowin' the same dirt for hundreds of years. I tell you what, ma'am, Texans aren't built for bowin'. It's been bred right out of us."

Brazos leveled a hard stare on Victor Considérant and shook his peppermint in the Frenchman's direction. "And aristocrats are just as bad as royalty. That fellow's one of the worst. Although I'll admit that his head's on right about kings and all, his whole notion to create a socialistic city in the heart of Texas is just plain stupid."

Gesturing toward the others who waited ahead of them in line, he said, "Look around you, lady. I'd lay odds not more than a dozen of these folks know the first little bit about farmin', much less what it takes for survivin' on the frontier. Take that crate, for instance." He shook his head incredulously, "They've stored work tools with violins for an ocean crossing, for goodness sake. These folks don't have the sense to pour rain water from a boot!" He popped the candy into his mouth, folded his arms across his chest, and studied the ship, chewing in a pensive silence.

The nerve of the man, Madeline thought, gritting her teeth against the words she'd love to speak. Really, to comment on another's intelligence when his own is so obviously lacking. Listen to his French.

And his powers of observation. Why, she knew how she looked.

Beautiful wasn't the appropriate word.

Brazos swallowed his candy and said, "Hmm. You've given me an idea." Before Madeline gathered her wits to stop him, he leaned over and kissed her cheek. "Thanks, Beauty. And listen, you take care out here without a man to protect you. If I see your husband on this boat I'm goin' to give him a piece of my mind about leavin' you alone." He winked and left her, walking toward the gangway.

Madeline touched the sticky spot on her cheek damp from his peppermint kiss and watched, fascinated despite herself, as the over-bold Texan tapped Considérant on the shoulder. In French that grated on her ears, he said. "Listen Frenchman, I'll make a deal with you. If you find a place for me on your ship I'll be happy to share my extensive knowledge of Texas with any of your folks who'd be interested in learnin'. This land you bought on the Trinity River—it's not more than half a day's ride from my cousin's spread. I've spent a good deal of time in that area over the past few years. I can tell you all about it."

"Mr. Sinclair," Considérant said in English, "please do not further abuse my language. I chose that land myself. Personally. I can answer any questions my peers may have about our new home. Now, as I have told you, this packet has been chartered to sail La Réunion colonists exclusively. Every space is assigned. I sympathize with your need to return to your home, but unfortunately the *Uriel* cannot accommodate you. Please excuse me, Monsieur Sinclair. I have much to see to before we sail. Good day."

"Good day my—" Brazos bit off his words. He turned abruptly and stomped away from the ship. Halting before Madeline, he declared, "This boat ain't leavin' until morning. It's not over yet. By General Taylor's tailor, when it sails, I'm gonna be on it."

He flashed a victorious grin and drawled, "Honey, you've captured my heart and about three other parts. I'll look forward to seein' you aboard ship."

As he walked away, she dropped a handsome gold pocket watch into her reticule, then called out to him in crisp, King's English. "Better you had offered your brain for ballast, Mr. Sinclair. Perhaps then you'd have been allowed aboard the *Uriel*."

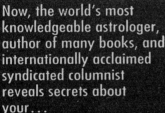

OFFICIAL RULES

To enter the sweepstakes below carefully follow all instructions found elsewhere this offer.

The **Winners Classic** will award prizes with the following approximate maximum values: 1 Grand Prize: $26,500 (or $25,000 cash alternate); 1 First Prize: $3,000; Second Prizes: $400 each; 35 Third Prizes: $100 each; 1,000 Fourth Prizes: $7.50 each. Total maximum retail value of Winners Classic Sweepstakes is $42,500. Some presentations of this sweepstakes may contain individual entry numbers corresponding to one or more of the aforementioned prize levels. To determine the Winners, individual entry numbers will first be compared with the winning numbers preselected by computer. For winning numbers not returned, prizes will be awarded in random drawings from among all eligible entries received. Prize choices may be offered at various levels. If a winner chooses an automobile prize, all license and registration fees, taxes, destination charges, and other expenses not offered herein are the responsibility of the winner. If a winner chooses a trip, travel must be complete within one year from the time the prize is awarded. Minors must be accompanied by an adult. Travel companion(s) must also sign release of liability. Trips are subject to space and departure availability. Certain black-out dates may apply.

The following applies to the sweepstakes named above:

No purchase necessary. You can also enter the sweepstakes by sending your name and address to: P.O. Box 508, Gibbstown, N.J. 08027. Mail each entry separately. Sweepstakes begins 6/1/93. Entries must be received by 12/30/94. Not responsible for lost, late, damaged, misdirected, illegible or postage due mail. Mechanically reproduced entries are not eligible. All entries become property of the sponsor and will not be returned.

Prize Selection/Validations: Selection of winners will be conducted no later than 5:00 PM on January 28, 1995, by an independent judging organization whose decisions are final. Random drawings will be held at 1211 Avenue of the Americas, New York, N.Y. 10036. Entrants need not be present to win. Odds of winning are determined by total number of entries received. Circulation of this sweepstakes is estimated not to exceed 200 million. All prizes are guaranteed to be awarded and delivered to winners. Winners will be notified by mail and may be required to complete an affidavit of eligibility and release of liability which must be returned within 14 days of date of notification or alternate winners will be selected in a random drawing. Any prize notification letter or any prize returned to a participating sponsor, Bantam Doubleday Dell Publishing Group, Inc., its participating divisions or subsidiaries, or the independent judging organization as undeliverable will be awarded to an alternate winner. Prizes are not transferable. No substitution for prizes except as offered or as may be necessary due to unavailability, in which case a prize of equal or greater value will be awarded. Prizes will be awarded approximately 90 days after the drawing. All taxes are the sole responsibility of the winners. Entry constitutes permission (except where prohibited by law) to use winners' names, hometowns, and likenesses for publicity purposes without further or other compensation. Prizes won by minors will be awarded in the name of parent or legal guardian.

Participation: Sweepstakes open to residents of the United States and Canada except for the province of Quebec. Sweepstakes sponsored by Bantam Doubleday Dell Publishing Group, Inc., (BDD), 1540 Broadway, New York, NY 10036. Versions of this sweepstakes with different graphics and prize choices will be offered in conjunction with various solicitations or promotions by different subsidiaries and divisions of BDD. Where applicable, winners will have their choice of any prize offered at level won. Employees of BDD, its divisions, subsidiaries, advertising agencies, independent judging organization, and their immediate family members are not eligible.

Canadian residents, in order to win, must first correctly answer a time limited arithmetical skill testing question. Void in Puerto Rico, Quebec and wherever prohibited or restricted by law. Subject to all federal, state, local and provincial laws and regulations. For a list of major prize winners (available after 1/29/95): send a self addressed, stamped envelope entirely separate from your entry to: Sweepstake Winners, P.O. Box 517, Gibbstown, NJ 08027. Requests must be received by 12/30/94. DO NOT SEND ANY OTHER CORRESPONDENCE TO THIS P.O. BOX.

Don't miss these fabulous Bantam women's fiction titles

now on sale

• NOTORIOUS
by Patricia Potter, author of *RENEGADE*
Long ago, Catalina Hilliard had vowed never to give away her heart, but she hadn't counted on the spark of desire that flared between her and her business rival, Marsh Canton. Now that desire is about to spin Cat's carefully orchestrated life out of control.
_____56225-8 $5.50/6.50 in Canada

• PRINCESS OF THIEVES
by Katherine O'Neal, author of *THE LAST HIGHWAYMAN*
Mace Blackwood was a daring rogue—the greatest con artist in the world. Saranda Sherwin was a master thief who used her wits and wiles to make tough men weak. And when Saranda's latest charade leads to tragedy and sends her fleeing for her life, Mace is compelled to follow, no matter what the cost.
_____56066-2 $5.50/$6.50 in Canada

• CAPTURE THE NIGHT
by Geralyn Dawson
In this "Once Upon a Time" Romance with "Beauty and the Beast" at its heart, Geralyn Dawson weaves the love story of a runaway beauty, the Texan who rescues her, and their precious stolen "Rose."
_____56176-6 $4.99/5.99 in Canada

Ask for these books at your local bookstore or use this page to order.

❑ Please send me the books I have checked above. I am enclosing $ _____ (add $2.50 to cover postage and handling). Send check or money order, no cash or C. O. D.'s please.

Name _____

Address _____

City/ State/ Zip _____

Send order to: Bantam Books, Dept. FN123, 2451 S. Wolf Rd., Des Plaines, IL 60018

Allow four to six weeks for delivery.

Prices and availability subject to change without notice.

FN123 12/93

Don't miss these fabulous Bantam women's fiction titles

on sale in December

- ### DESIRE by Amanda Quick, *New York Times*
bestselling author of DECEPTION
"Quick has provided an inviting little world...A featherlight, warmhearted fantasy...Fans will welcome this perfect little pop-over of a romance."—Kirkus Reviews___ 56153-7 $5.99/$6.99 *in Canada*

- ### LONG TIME COMING
by Sandra Brown, *New York Times* bestselling author of *Temperatures Rising* and *French Silk*
"Ms. Brown's larger than life heroes and heroines make you believe in all the warm, wonderful, wild things in life."
—Rendezvous ___ 56278-9 $4.99/$5.99 *in Canada*

- ### ALL MY SINS REMEMBERED
by Rosie Thomas
"A compelling and moving story...full of wisdom and caring."
—The Washington Post Book World___ 56368-8 $5.99/$6.99 n *Canada*

- ### STRANGER IN MY ARMS by R. J. Kaiser
With no recollection of who she was, Hillary Bass became spellbound by a love she couldn't resist...and haunted by a murder she couldn't recall... ___ 56251-7 $4.99/$5.99 *in Canada*

- ### WHERE DOLPHINS GO by Peggy Webb
She was a mother looking for a miracle, he was a doctor looking to forget. The last thing they expected was to find each other.
___ 56056-5 $5.99/$6.99 n *Canada*

Ask for these books at your local bookstore or use this page to order.

❑ Please send me the books I have checked above. I am enclosing $ _____ (add $2.50 to cover postage and handling). Send check or money order, no cash or C. O. D.'s please.

Name _____

Address _____

City/ State/ Zip _____

Send order to: Bantam Books, Dept. FN124, 2451 S. Wolf Rd., Des Plaines, IL 60018
Allow four to six weeks for delivery.

Prices and availability subject to change without notice. FN124 12/93